Blood & HONOR

BY

CHAVEZ MOORE

ISBN: 978-1-951300-41-8

Liberation's Publishing – West Point - Mississippi

Blood

&HONOR

CONTENTS

DRAMATIS PERSONAE

Main Characters

Sebak Daivari (Kush Warrior reincarnation of a powerful Warrior)
Alessia (Huntress Suebi Warrioress/A Shaman)
Neville (Brother to Alessia)

Important Side Characters

Monk Powle (Another father figure to Sebak)
Sir Edger Roland (well respected knight/Step-father to Sebak &
husband to Malin)
Mal (An old Man seeming to be on a path of redemption)
Scar (An old Naga Warrior that Vowed to protect Sebak with his life)
Malin Daivari (Adopted Mother of Sebak)

PROLOGUE

There were no signs, and it came without warning. a light that engulfed the world. A desperate few struggled to survive. Perhaps we had a chance for peace, but desperation and trust are seldom align. So began three centuries of conflict. Emperor Morkere of Sayari decided he wanted the world. Twenty years of war had begun, the greatest warriors the world has ever known arose. Emperor claimed all our homes within those years. He achieved that of which many believed was impossible and conquered the four other kingdoms in Sayari. Those that sought peace were subjugated to the emperor making him successful in conquering their world. As for me and my family we were born and chains for different reasons. We were made to fight by the emperor because our people did not believe in his ways. My mother died giving birth to me in this harsh world.

As for my father he died in the Colosseum giving these greedy people a show. I am made to do as my father did giving these people a show as a gladiator and die for their amusement. All to protect my clan who I have never met in my twenty years of life. I am Sebak Daivari the last of my line. If I am to do anything with my life, it is to get out of these chains living as I see fit until it's time for me to return to the earth

Greed shaped the world into something dark and vile. A place where many did not recognize it any more. Survival was always our main goal in life but politics and war has made it difficult for many. Nomadic tribes were hunted down by the kingdom's soldiers for not changing their ways. Everything had to be how the emperor and his senate wanted it to be. Slavery and trade became the most profitable way to make money. Along with many other ungodly things that humanity has created for themselves. "I want to change all of that and watch the world burn…"

CHAPTER 1: A RISE OF A SHADOW

Our story begins with young Sebak's entry into the world. "I love you my son but I must give you away. You will have a better life here with these humans than with me." she sails him down a river in a basket that she woven herself in secret. This was the first time ever that the Queen had ever cried for anything in her life. watching her child float away front of her eyes. Moments later, he washes ashore towards a small village. A young woman named Malin sees the basket and curiously opens it without hesitation. "Oh, what a strange child this is." Malin says to herself. "A wooly haired man child! His hair is as white as snow." White as snow it was, unique to any one in his tribe of people. It was perplexing against his beautiful brown skin and brown eyes.

She looks around to see if she could discover where the child has come from but no sign of anything or anyone. Malin thinks that someone did not want their child or something horrible has happened to them. She picks up the little one as he warms up in her arms from her body heat. "Oh, you are cold little one. How long have you been in that basket?" as she uses her clothing to cover him up in. When she picks up Sebak she discovers that he has a note that was with him. it was mostly ruined by the water that entered the basket.

The note read, "Please! Whoever you are I would

ask you to take care of my son Sebak. He is the most precious thing I have in this world. he is the only precious thing I have in this world. He is not like the rest of his race. He is more than that. He is something special. I ask that you treat him like your own and rase him to become a man. So, one day he can find me if I still live. I love you my son, the Queen." Malin did not know what to make of it all. But she now knew the baby's name. His name was Sebak and he was of noble birth apparently. She tells the little one while he smiles at her, "I will always love you. I will always be here for you."

Sebak's life had a wonderful beginning, and he grew in wisdom of the gods. he was far advanced in years and his family, and the people of Ashfield loved him dearly. None really wondered or cared where Sebak truly had come from. They all believed that he was a blessing from the gods that they did not deserve to have.

It was early morning, before sunrise when the emperor's soldiers arrived in the land of Ashfield. Sebak awoke to shrieks, screams, and the sound of shackles being locked upon the hands and feet of many. He saw the strongest of his people beaten into submission. Families were being torn apart. He peered through the tent curtains as he saw a young girl's mom fall in despair as her daughter was carried away in a cart with complete strangers. She had tried to run behind the carriage but could not keep up. Her daughter was gone. "Get up!" A soldier yelled, whipping her in one motion upon his shoulders. She yelled and beat his back to no avail. He threw her into a cart that went in the opposite direction. "What is happening momma?" Sebak asked his mom as she responded. Amid the turmoil and screams Sebak and his mom held on to each other tightly as they tried to hide under the hay and covers within their home.

"This is the last tent to check sir!" a soldier called out as he headed into the place where Sebak and his mother hid. Another voice arose, "Ill check here knight you go ahead and prepare my cart." It was the voice of Sir Edgar Roland, a knight with impeccable honor. He swept the room, and they were found out. The terror in Malin's eyes as she pleaded for her son with them caught the heart of Sir Roland. "Come." He said, extending his hand to them both. "I will not separate you, you will both accompany me." He responded as he gazed at Sebak with silent contemplation. It was Sebak's uniqueness that saved them, for in Sir Roland's mind Sebak must be blessed by the gods to have snow white hair at such a young age. Malin's beauty and the way she held the young child only added to his amazement.

Sir Edger would later decide to make Malin his wife and save both of their lives. He would not touch Sebak's mother unless needed to. He would not dishonor her in any way. Edger would come home and sleep in a chair or on the floor to keep his new wife from feeling uncomfortable. He would treat her with his utmost respect every day no matter what kind of day he was having. Sir Edger would also spend a lot of time with Sebak when he had free time. He would teach him chess and how to use a weapon to teach the lad how to survive in this world. Wanting the boy to have a chance in this harsh and greedy world that he was born into. Over time he would learn that this child is very special in his own way. Sebak at a young age showed that he was remarkably intelligent in all things chess once his step father taught him.

The lad would often have issues sleeping at night. He would have bad dreams he would call them. Malin dismissed them as just bad dreams and thought nothing of them. But Sir edger knew exactly what they were. Sebak was having visions of the future randomly and not just of his future. He was seeing multiple people's outcomes, people he didn't know or people he would meet. Sir Edger knew he had to suppress this somehow so no one thinks his step-son is a sorcerer or something. One night he goes into the boy's bedroom and use's holy magic to help him. This only shows Edger what the boy was seeing. Sir Edger realized that Sebak was chosen.

Many of the knights that would visit Sir Edger would think that Sebak and his mother were the help and could be treated anyway they saw fit. But the moment Sir Edger saw the horrible manner they were treating them he banished them from his home. This is the second time Sebak sees the evil in this world and Sir

Edger was there to put an end to it this time. Sebak protected his mother like a man should do when the father is not around. Sir Edger tells the boy, "Good job son. That is what a son should do for his mother. You have spunk young one." Edger was proud of Sebak and believed that he could be something one day.

"Honor… what do you know about honor? You… who never faced true fear learn what honor is before pretending you are a warrior. Know this… before you step on to that thin red path where no misstep is allowed. A path that only ends when your legs fail to support you and when your heart stops beating. A path where sadness goes along with pain and where glory is the color of blood. This narrow path goes only one way. A way covered with enemies and brothers and it will take you without any shame into the hands of death for the name you were given and for your descendants." Edger tells Sebak all of his life.

From that moment Sebak would think of those words that his step father told him for years. Things would be okay for the family from that point on. Edger would stop being friends with some of the soldiers that were racist or thought low of his wife and step son. In all of that time Sir Edger would spend time with both of them. Making the most of a once bad situation and giving them a better life. Malin eventually grows to love Edger because of his kind heart. He would often tell them he will always be there for them no matter what happens. Even training Sebak at a young age in the way of the blade. When the lad turns sixteen is when trouble arrived once again for them.

Because the lad was showing such promise to become a knight some of the soldiers wanted to sabotage the lad's future. Sir Edger was training the young man to become a knight from what the others were thinking. They did not want someone of his kind among their ranks. At first the Warden of Sonia did not care about what they young boy wanted to become. Only people of noble birth could become a knight according to their laws. With that being said the soldiers that were once Sir Edger's friends started to plot against him. Stuck in their ways they prefer to keep people like Sebak under their boot than allow them to make a name for themselves. So, they purposely send their children to mess with the lad.

Some of the children actually liked hanging out with Sebak because of how intelligent he was. But all it took was one person to change the lad's life for good. One day Sebak and a few other children were playing outside the walls. Kids being kids they saw Sebak stare at the noble sisters named Emilia. They tried to set the two of them up because both were looking at one another often. This was not the first time that the two would do such a thing. They would often spend time talking to one another when everyone else went home. One day Emilia asked to meet Sebak alone after they stopped playing with their friends. He meets her then everything fell apart for him in the matter of seconds. It wasn't Emilia that met him that day it was her sister Evilly and she sent the knights on him.

Sir Edger & Malin hear of the situation and tries at their best to defend their son. Edger would even give up his rank to save his step-son's life. The Warden of Seonia decides that the boy must go to the gladiator arena and serve until he is released. As for Sir Edger he was to serve ten years on a crusade for redemption. This was the simplest punishment the Warden wanted to deal out having already made his decision before the parents arrived. This angered Sir Edger in every way possible but he did what he was told. Not before he had to say goodbye to Sebak before going on his crusade. This is before the Emperor of Zetopia extended his rule to them and changed the knights for Roman Legionaries. Considering Knight hood as an old and dying practice.

Sebak was forced into the pits at the age of sixteen and was told every fight he won would serve in taking care of his mother. For every fight they would give his mother some silver or gold depending on the fights and if he won. On his first fight he was full of fear and hate for what has happened to his family. But he had to survive for his mother's sake considering Sir Edger would be gone for ten years.

Sebak at first was not a great gladiator but he made his way work for himself and his mother. But in these pits Honor was hard to hold on to. Taking a life at the age of sixteen was traumatizing for the young lad. He had to do so to survive in the pits. Eventually he made it to the colosseum and became one of the best fighters. It took him a year before he was better than most. Some believe he had some divine intervention for him to survive for this long. Sebak only was surviving because of his faith and his sword arm. He had to remember what Edger had taught him when he was younger to help him learn quicker. The men in charge would often talk about a great gladiator that would never be beaten around Sebak. How that young man would soon be free if he stayed undefeated. This was what he had to learn how to do survive and become undefeated. He saw this undefeated gladiator as a rival to outmatch him.

The lad would watch the others fight in the arena. He would study them all even though he would barely win his fights. He needed to get better and the only way to do so was to practice. He used this time to look at his chess pieces that he keeps in a bag under his bed. He used them to point out the people in power and how he was only a pawn for now. He needed to become the first black Knight. He thought favor would begin there if it was anywhere in this world. A knight commanded respect to all those in his presence. In the meantime, the gladiators would be visited by monks that would pray for them often. One was not what he seemed and picked Sebak out of the group to train.

The lad's style meant that he was not an attraction to the crowd. They hoped he would die in one of these opening games. But this mysterious Monk would show up every so often to train Sebak in his cultural ways.

Sebak didn't understand why he chose him until one day he asked the monk. One day during training he asked, "Why me? I'm nothing special. I don't even think I'll ever make it out of these pits. All I can do is make sure my mother is safe."

The monk only looked at the lad and corrected his stances. He did not intend to answer the lad yet. All the monk would tell him was, "Even the smallest ripple could change the flow." Often the riddles from the monk would confuse him but he continued to train and found peace in the dances the monk showed him. Peace like he would find under a waterfall listening to nature. He would dream of going into the woods and listening to the birds singing and watching the animals in their natural habitats. The monk would correct him knocking him out of these fantasies. But he missed swimming in the oceans and the ponds. It was something soothing about being under the water. Then one day the monk told the lad that his training was done. From here on you will have to practice on your own. Sebak was confused until he heard the soldiers talking about how Sebak was to fight soon.

He realized that the monk was only spending time with him because he was not fighting for months. These months was enough to help Sebak learn a new flow of motion and how to understand his opponents from the monk. Many things the monk taught him seemed weird but he learned them anyway. Because it was not his place to question it but to learn from what he can to survive in these pits. At the same time, he wondered how his mother was fairing because he hasn't fought for months. He often would get letters from her telling him that she is okay and she would be there every time for Sebak's fights even though she dislikes the colosseum. She would stomach anything for her son.

Then for the first time in few months Sebak was to fight a well-trained gladiator one on one. Everyone was there for this event because their champions were to fight later on. Sebak and the other gladiator waited for the emperor's approval and then began their fight as the roaring of the crowd began. Sebak could see the weakness in his opponent was movement. So, he shredded armor so he could move quicker.

By outsmarting his opponent, he beat him quickly getting the people to cheer for him. The feeling was different for Sebak altogether. Because of Sebak's training he became a more disciplined warrior. He felt like his training was finally complete. This was not the only decisive victory that Sebak would get. He would go on to win many fights giving his mother a lot of money to take care of herself. It only took a matter of months for Sebak to become a champion at the age of seventeen. He started to understand a little of what the monk saw in him. He could see that the boy was a survivor and a strategist. To Sebak the arena became his training grounds and he did not even know it yet. Months pass and he started using his brain to survive encounters and strategize against his opponents.

Unlike most people that usually get cocky after winning he became more disciplined with every victory. It started to annoy some of the people that put him in the pits in the first place. But everyone could see that Sebak was starting to blossom in the colosseum. He became the reason many of the other gladiators survived military reenactments. Sebak gets the attention of the Emperor of Sayari. He would not allow for Sebak's freedom because he had to serve the years promised. The emperor does give the boy a way out of this though. He tells him, "In six-years' time he will bring his champion for a major event. If you can defeat him in battle then you can go free. Sebak agrees to this and that he would be ready for the undefeated gladiator.

Time passes and Sebak continues to do what the monk trained him to do. Sebak earns favor from the emperor and he is granted one weapon to make him feel like a champion. At the age of eighteen he was given a curved hilted sword by the emperor and he has used this weapon in every fight sense receiving it. By the age of twenty he was given another weapon choice for being undefeated for so long. Sebak decides to have his own weapon forged that he believed suited his style.

He was given the chance to forge his own weapon by the emperor and he chose to forge two silver swords as one weapon making it a double-sided & double-bladed sword. This weapon was the first of its kind in their world and everyone believed it was a weird weapon to forge. Because of its size and the two blades they didn't think it was possible to use. But Sebak proved them wrong on many occasions with the weapon because of his training he became a deadly figure with the weapon. The Wardens would often ban the weapon from being used because they want to see a fair fight. Even though Sebak's odds are never fair for him. He begins defying the Wardens and becoming a huge problem for them. So, they plot to kill him in any way possible they could think of. Assassination was even attempted and Sebak overcame it. Then the wardens come up with a plan to kill Sebak once and for all. They manipulate the emperor into sending the Praetorian guard to kill Sebak because he has defied the emperor's rule.

Seeing they were trying to manipulate him he confronts the Wardens telling them to watch their steps because he will not be manipulated. But he sends the guards anyway because Sebak has become a problem because the people are behind him. this could result in a rebellion so the emperor wanted no part in the Warden's sick games.

Sebak readies himself to enter the colosseum for the twentieth time in his life. Throughout his time as a gladiator the Wardens of Seonia & Brithia has been trying to break him. Ever sense the young lad has arrived into his colosseum he has been defiant. The crowd grew to love the lad quickly after every victory Sebak received. Each bought gave him his fair share of scars mentally and physically. The Warden Sir Jeremy loved breaking people's spirits any way he could. He has used everything in his power to break the young man, even going as far as using his family against him. He separated the young lad from his entire family when he was of age to become a gladiator.

Ever sense Sebak grew to be more of a thorn in his side every day. While the people grew to love the young boy. But this time they had it out for the boy and wanted him to battle alone against twenty praetorian guards. The emperor believed that this would be good training for his men considering Sebak was the best among the gladiators. This would also get rid of the problems Warden Jeremy was having with him. The emperor sent more than just twenty guards; the others were to protect the Warden if things were to get out of hand with the people once Sebak had been killed. The crowd did not appreciate their favorite gladiator facing such odds.

So, to motivate everyone in the arena and make the games more interesting Warden Jeremy tells two gladiators that if they killed Sebak, they would have their freedom. Among the twenty praetorian guards were two of the best gladiators in the world. When the fight began Sebak was highly outnumbered and he did not have his signature weapon because of the Wardens banning the weapon. When the engagement began one of the gladiators throws Sebak his signature weapon named "Sting" (double-bladed Sword). With this act of treachery towards the Wardens the Praetorian guards kill the gladiator for his defiance. The other gladiator begins to fight the guards as well dying to give Sebak a chance. Because of this Sebak was able to fight off the guard with difficulty because of their training. Once he unbalanced them with his unorthodox ways they were defeated.

But this helped Sir Jeremy's cause because as the other gladiators died for Sebak they yelled, "For the cause" and it helped uncover a possible rebellion. This made Warden Jeremy smile because now they must warn the emperor of an imminent rebellion if they do not kill Sebak or cleanse this eventual uprising. Upon doing so the emperor does nothing but smile at the Warden.

He tells him, "I already knew of the uprising. Why do you think I armed Sebak with hope of getting free of his predicament? It'll all be handled when the boy fights my champion. Then the potential rebels will lose their champion and hope all at the same time." So, the Emperor allows this to go on for years so he can rule out the people against him. the Warden wanted to find a way to crush Sebak's spirit before the big event. The only way he knew how to hurt the young man was his mother. Before everyone knew it ten years had passed by. This meant the return of Sir Edger Roland and none of the soldiers were happy about it. But everyone in the kingdom was prepared for that knight's return. They even had a plan up their sleeves on what to do about him once he returned to the castle.

When he returned to meet his wife Malin on the

bridge, he saw her smiling face once again after ten years of waiting. The two hug one another and kiss each other to show their affection for one another. Not long after Malin is shot by an arrow in the chest. Edger had put his guard down for only a moment to be happy and it cost him. It was happening as he feared it would and he was naive enough to think he could have a normal life. Sir Edger had to suck up his tears because he would have to tell his step son what has happened to his mother. That would be harder than watching her die in front of his eyes. Only because it will be like she has died twice because he would have to see Sebak break down from the news of his mother's death.

The colosseum was packed this year because of the prize fight in the end. Many were there to see undefeated champions battle it out for everything. Even a young woman named Alessia was present for this event scouting for Sir Edger's signal. Her brother was up top watching his sister's back for this mission. The sheer numbers in the arena alone would tell anyone coming in that this would be a one-time event of the year. Something their Emperor has decided to do for his people.

Sir Edger had to bring the news to Sebak before his fight. The two of them did not imagine their reunion to be like this. The news broke Sebak in ways a person should never experience. Edger couldn't embrace his step son because of the bars between them. Edger wanted to help him breathe but he couldn't do so physically, all he could do was try to talk him into breathing. Sebak threw the biggest tantrum he has ever done sense he was a child. He began throwing things and blaming himself. Edger would tell him, "They were going to kill one of use eventually. They could not kill the warriors so they went after the people we love to hurt us. Do not let them win son. Don't let them gain the power over you. I loved your mother with all of my heart and she was my world. You have an enemy to face son and u must do it with your mind together. They took our heart from us by eliminating our connection through your mother."

"Show them that they are wrong for hurting us. Show them the tiger I know that is within you. Show them you will not bow and you will not break son." Empowering his son was all he could do before his fight. Because he knew the pain he must be feeling. It hurt Sir Edger a lot because he could not be there for his step son. His face must anger him because as soon as he arrived terrible things began to happen once again to their family. When will it all end for them both of them thought in their grief? But Sebak had to get his mind set for the arena because no one in the arena would grant him mercy because his mother is dead.

In his mind he had nothing but sadness and rage filled thoughts. He did not know what was the right thing to do anymore. He quickly thought about if it was not for him, she would not have been in this situation and they would not be burying her right now. "This all my fault!" is that was no his mind right now. He was starting to lose his sanity because if it wasn't for him then this possibly would not have happened. He had to sit down with his hands upon his head and his head down to not let anyone see him crying.

CHAPTER 2 BLOOD FOR FREEDOM

"A man can have anything if he is willing to sacrifice. With your birth comes a solum vow that you will have nothing. A person's privilege is the dirt. I've seen it, and it is nothing short of truth. I have dealt with the worst and have endured what many before me have . I am nothing is what they try to teach me. They are wrong. I am more than nothing and I will prove them wrong. I will rise where others have fallen." Sebak thought on these things while being on his on after learning from Sir Edger and the monk. All that he has learned led him to this moment. He thinks, "If I am to die today then let me be … No! I am not dying today and my story does not end here. My story will become legendary one day. The gladiator that defied a nation

Sebak enters the arena ready with his weapons to meet his fate. He sticks his curved hilted sword into the ground readying himself for the fight to come. But then the announcer introduced the champion they all have been waiting for. The entire evening was betting on this fight to be one for the ages. Sebak recognizes the man across from him the second he stepped his foot out. It was the monk that trained him in secret. He now understood what was going on. He had been in service to the emperor sense his family was defeated by him. The old man wanted to be released from this oath. The only way he could be released from a family oath is death.

The young man did not know if he could kill someone that he looks up to. But he has to for his story to continue. The monk tells him, "I will not hesitate to kill you boy." As he readies his spear to fight his old apprentice. Sebak readies his trusted weapon Sting to battle his old teacher. Then the Emperor stops them and says he changes his mind on how this event will go. First the boy must make it past the Praetorian guards that killed his mother for starting a rebellion. Then he can fight two of my champions at the same time. This will be a day to remember where we are entertained like no other.

The monk is then accompanied by five guards and a female gladiator. The two champions would rather old their fight after the guards is killed. Sebak fights the guards and their wall that they tried to make. The female champion starts to get restless and runs for the fight. But she is stopped by the monk and they begin to battle. The emperor did not expect to see two fights at the same time. He did not want his champions fighting one another but he could not stop them either. Sebak makes short work of the guards because of his maneuverability. Then he enters the fight of champions they called it.

Once they all were in the fight, it became a three-way battle. The Monk and the female gladiator have been rivals for years and never got to fight. This was their chance to show their inner aggression towards one another. But they were getting paid to kill the boy Sebak and work as a team. They worked most of their issues out before Sebak entered the battle. Then the two proceeded to fight him together slowly. The monk's expression throughout the entire thing never changed. He seemed cold to what was happening in this battle, seeming almost emotionless on the fight. With Sting at his side Sebak was able to stave off any attack thrown at him almost. Until the Monk found an opening to kick the boy away.

The female gladiator leaped to attack Sebak with her trident but he was quick enough to dodge her. The Monk also attacked Sebak to catch him off-guard but to no avail. Sebak seemed to be able to see all their moves before they made it. On the inside the Monk seemed proud of the young man and he cracks a smile at Sebak. He knocks the Monk off balance for the first time ever and knocks him down. Leaving Sebak to fight the female gladiator one on one. The two block each other left and right Sebak went on the defensive against the woman. He lets her disarm him so she could feel confident about her advance. He allowed her to have a sense of victory for only a second. Using the moment to flowingly dance behind her and snap her neck.

The Monk full on smiled after seeing Sebak smoothly take down the other champion. As her body hits the ground the crowd goes quiet and the emperor is surprised by this. The two of them stared each other down for a second as the crowd was shocked at what just transpired. The Monk drops the spear to engage Sebak hand to hand. The crowd had never seen anything on this scale before and was on the edge of their seats. People began betting on the two of the remaining Champions. Many bet that Sebak would win this fight while others that gotten rich off of the Monk stayed true to their bet from the start.

The emperor getting uptight about the situation signals the entertainers for something. The fight escalated quickly as they open trap doors for tigers to come out of the ground. They were chained up and their mission was to keep the Champions fighting one another. The Monk then taught Sebak something while they were fighting. The boy learned quickly on how to put the tigers down without hurting them. The Monk does it first then Sebak does it after him when each were close to being attacked. They hit a pressure point on the tigers to put them to sleep.

Then the Monk kicks the trident from the ground into the air and then follows it up with a second kick to launch the weapon at Sebak. Sebak dodges the attack and see that the Monk rearmed himself with his spear. So, he grabs his curved hilted sword that was sticking out of the ground the entire time. Both lunge at one another and begin to clash their weapons. Meanwhile, the Monk finally breaks his silence, "I am proud of you Sebak. You have become greater than I expected you to be. Your discipline is something to be proud of. You may become greater than you expect. But you must get past me you only obstacle right now. Have you figured out the riddle yet?" He says to him whispering in his ear. Sebak did not know if he was messing with him to knock him off balance or not. But he wasn't going to easily fall for it keeping his guard up at all times.

But Sebak could sense the sincerity in his voice meaning that he was not lying to him. Everyone could sense the ending coming soon and did not know who would win the overall battle. The two fought with all of their being in this fight to see who would be the victor. Just when it seemed that all was lost for Sebak he finally gets the upper hand on the Monk. He disarms the monk only to slice his arm and his leg on the same side to knock him down. But Sebak could not bring himself to kill the monk. He was a mentor to him for months on end and would give him advice on almost everything. The crowd chanted for him to kill the Monk even the emperor gave his approval for the monk to die.

This motion angered Sebak because the monk had given his life to serving the emperor. Sebak yells at the emperor on his pedestal, "That is how you treat your devoted followers? How can anyone call you lord or Emperor? Are they so underneath you that you do not care for them?" The emperor responds, "Because he knew his place. He was my entertainment and he has finally lost. So, he must die for disappointing me. In fact, everyone here knows their place except you. I protect them and the nobles make their money off of little people like you. You have not figured out that you are only a foot not boy. Now kill him so we all can go home." This angers Sebak beyond belief that someone could be so cold towards another's life.

For every person that Sebak has killed he prayed for before and after their fights even if they were difficult. He never believed it was their fault that they had to battle. They were put against one another to survive in this dark world. Sebak saved those he could by being merciful to many of his opponents throughout the years. He killed those that did not seem to understand where he was coming from. But this man that they call the emperor had no remorse for anyone that was in his care. The people did not matter to him and he believes he can do what he likes with anyone's life. He must be stopped before this can go on any longer.

The Monk could read what Sebak was about to do and mouthed to him, "If you attempt anything everyone will try to kill you, even me." Sebak paused and looked down at the blood on his hands thinking of all that has happened to him in his short life. Everything that has happened to him were because of corrupt people like him. He wants to live his own life without someone else manipulating him. A decision popped into his head and he did not share it with anyone not even the Monk. But unimaginable rage overtook Sebak to the point that the young man's eyes changed color. His original eye color being brown and they changed to a light yellow.

Sebak grabs his curved hilted sword and charges at the pedestal that the emperor was on. The tigers awaken at the same time that he charges as if he woke them up. He uses one of them to jump higher than any human has ever accomplished. He shocked the world with this maneuver as the guards jump to protect the emperor. But it was too late. Sebak was on his neck before anyone had realized what happened. He caught the emperor completely off-guard and he could not react in time.

The only one capable of reacting in time was the Monk and he managed to grab a whip that was long enough to catch Sebak. It catches him right before he achieved his killing blow. The Monk pulls him back down to him as the crowd was terrified of what just transpired. Sebak manages to leave a mark on the emperor's cheek as he is pulled back. The guards then get the emperor as they watch what transpired. He also picks up a sword from one of the dead guards as Sebak was coming back down. He knew the rules of how things were to go. He now had to be killed for attempting to kill the emperor. But unbelievably Sebak lands on his feet once he reaches the ground and engages the Monk quickly. They clash twice before the unthinkable happened. Sebak in anger slices the Monk's stomach open during the engagement. He didn't see that move coming because of the way it was executed and his sword was above the attack.

Once Sebak turns around he realizes what he has done

to his mentor. But the old man was smiling when Sebak turned around. He drops the sword and to his knees to fall over. Sebak then let's go of his rage and drops his weapon to catch the Monk before he hit the ground. He embraces the Monk and starts to drop tears. The Monk tells him, "Are those for me? Do not be sad. I am happy… Thank you my friend." As he closes his eyes and passes away peacefully. He could not believe what he had done. Because he had already granted him mercy only to be killed a second later. He felt that he just breached his honorable ways by doing this. He always thought of himself as an honest man and to kill someone like this was not right.

The emperor being embarrassed by a peasant in front of his friends was not going to stand. He tells the soldiers to kill the gladiator for striking him and the crowd booed the emperor's choice. The chaos ensued after this command. The woman Alessia starts a riot with the people holding some of the soldiers back. While Sir Edger breaks into the pits to release the gladiators. This starts a rebellion very quickly and the emperor is not surprised that Sir Edger was with the rebellion. He knew he was surrounded by traitors but he did not know how many it was and they all showed their faces at one time. He gives the soldiers order to kill all of the gladiators.

Sir Edger takes this chance to get Sebak on a horse and make a break for freedom. First, he had to snap Sebak out of the sadness that was taking him over. The two rushes to the bridge to safety from the guards. There was fighting all around the city and the civilians were running for their lives. The gladiators that were released did as they pleased before the soldiers cut them down. Sebak looked around realizing what he was caged in the pits with. People that lost their humanity years ago and would do anything for themselves. But there were a few that were with Sir Edger and was helping them escape.

Then their horses were shot down before getting to the bridge. Leaving them backed into a corner and having to fight. Sebak would not leave his step-father behind like this. Sir Edger tells him, "If you do not escape then it was for nothing. Get out of her son. GO!" But Sebak could not make himself leave the person that taught him almost everything he knows. The Gladiators hold the line against the soldiers as they argued. The two of them fought alongside these unlikely heroes. Then from nowhere Alessia arrived to help them escape. There was only room for one and Sir Edger wanted it to be Sebak. Everyone that was willing to die for him knew what he could become. Time was running out and the draw bridge was raising. So Sebak gets on her horse and they ride away.

He looks back to watch his Step-father and the gladiators fight for his survival. They hold the soldiers back for a long time. Giving Alessia & Sebak enough time to get very far ahead of the soldiers. Once outside the city they meet up with Alessia's brother Neville, she calls him. But his name is a lot longer and way more complicated. He meets them with an extra horse and Sebak jumps onto his own horse. The three of them ride away and never look back. They don't stop riding until it was dark. Sebak's heart is filled with remorse and sorrow for the people he has lost today. He leaves everything behind in that city even the weapons. He leaves that entire life behind.

Meanwhile, Sir Edger is fighting to the last man inside

the city walls. The soldiers were nothing to him as he cut them down left and right. Gladiators fall around him as he does not give up on his step son. He would fight until there was nothing left in him and keep fighting. All to give Sebak a chance at a new life. He kills soldiers left and right until the emperor's guest stops him. A Khan from a world that they do not know of slices him down catching him off guard cutting Sir Edger's helmet down the middle. He falls to his knees and then hits the ground.

Sebak knew that his step father was gone from that point on. Once the killing blow was done, he felt it in his heart that he had lost another loved one. That night Sebak did not speak to either Alessia or Neville. The two of them understood that they were strangers to him. they did not engage him until they felt like he was approachable. But they could understand his pain of losing all their loved ones in one day. The two of them would talk about their past to make Sebak feel better about himself. How their family was destroyed by that monster of an Emperor for nothing at all. Their people were nomads and did not bother anyone.

Alessia was a short muscular-like woman with red hair, she was wearing leather clothes with a bow and quiver of arrows on her back. She also seemed to be armed with some daggers from what Sebak could see. He could tell she was a very headstrong person but caring on the inside. Neville on the other hand was her brother and muscular as well, he also was wearing leather clothes. But he was armed with six javelins and a version of a buckler shield. He was very different from his sister seeming more charismatic than she was. The two did not know what to do for Sebak because his whole entire world has been turn upside down in the matter of minutes.

But they had to keep moving to their people and they could not trust each other on this journey. This journey would be all about trusting one another considering they will be hunted every step of the way. Alessia didn't want to make the first move but knew someone had to break the silence. Sebak did nothing but sit with his knees to his chest and his arms crossed. He starred at the fire because he did not know what to do anymore. Alessia goes to touch Sebak and before she does Neville decides to talk to him and gets his attention.

.

CHAPTER 3: THE STRANGERS

Neville starts introducing himself and his sister properly to Sebak so he wouldn't feel alone. That night was weird for the three of them because Sir Edger paid them to save Sebak. But now it seems like they have been inserted into something huge. The next morning, they traveled to a nearby town. This small town was not noticeable and not on the map. Many come here to hide from the crown and others that are chasing them. Alessia believed that this would be a good idea to hide in this small town. Sebak senses that they have someone tailing them but cannot tell who it is. Once they go into town the person tailing them backs down from following. Realizing this he tells the others what was happening behind them without making any sudden moves.

The town was very dirty and many of the people were rude. Crime was happening openly on the street and people were being attack. The three of them were uneasy about where they were and wanted to move on from this town. They go into the tavern to find the bartender, so they could ask directions. Neville tries to ask him politely where the nearest city was and so on. But the bartender did not pay him any attention because of the way he was talking. Sebak scouted the area without moving and noticed not many people were in the tavern. There were a few men with tattoos on their arms and an old man sitting in the corner. Alessia moves Neville out of the way to talk to the bartender. She gets his attention with force making him face her.

This gets the attention of the men with tattoos on their arms as the bartender is under their gang's protection. Sebak notices this and taps Alessia that they have company coming up fast. The bartender continued to disrespect them until Alessia puts a knife to his throat. When he said something derogatory to her, she puts to his private area so he would talk. The tattooed men walk up on the three of them and they tell Alessia to put the bartender down because he was under their protection.

Neville was not happy with what Alessia has done and drawing attention to them. Alessia says to the men, *"Oh really? Now who is going to protect you from me for getting into my business?"* Confused the men start to laugh not intimidated by Alessia at all. The men laughing sets Alessia off with her anger fairly quickly. She puts the bartender down back in his spot and then stabs the bartender in the hand. She tells him, *"Hold this."* As she turns around and punches the closest guy to her. This begins a bar fight that Neville and Sebak were attempting to avoid. It was over as quick as it started because the thugs did not expect them to be trained fighters. The old man in the corner claps his hands as they finish beating them down. The bartender tries to remove the knife from his hand and Alessia knocks him out. The old man tells them his name is Mal an old pirate that retired from that life. He also gives them advice on how to avoid the main kingdoms and towns.

Alessia tells him, *"Thanks for your help. But we had it under control."* Mal responds, *"You did not need help... you just wanted to beat them up because you know what they have done to women. You wanted to feel like you were doing the world a favor."* He says with a grin. She was surprised that he could figure that out so easily. The old man was well built physically and was not armed with anything but his walking stick. Many would not think that he was a threat. But nothing was as it seemed in the town already. There was no law apparently and people could do what they wanted. It was outright chaos in the town and no one was doing anything about it.

Mal walked closely towards Sebak because he could sense something about him. Sebak on the other hand felt something was off about Mal and could tell he was not a pirate. Mal offers to lead them out of the town and they were okay with this. As leave the tavern Alessia gets her knife back from the bartender and she calls him a punk. He starts to wake and she knocks him out once again to make herself feel better.

The group grew uneasy as the old man walked with them outside of the town. Sebak could not help but feel like he knew who Mal was. It was a warm feeling about him that he could not place. Everyone was skeptical of the new person traveling with them. Once they are outside of the town, Mal was the first to break the silence by saying that he knows of their journey and would like to accompany them. He tells them, *"If you would have me on your journey, I could teach you youngsters a lot."* At first, they were undecided about him but he would then insist that he would be a good asset to their journey.

The four of them walk for many miles on horseback and then Alessia believes they are lost. The three of them look at their map and started to think that they did not know which way to go. But Mal knew exactly which way to go. He knew where they were going and everything. This made Alessia feel uncomfortable with Mal. So, she asked him, *"Who are you, old man? Are you going to be a problem?"* Mal starts to laugh at her and says, *"Easy young one I am not your enemy. Besides you could not kill me because stronger men have tried and I am still here."* He asks them to trust him because he could get them their safely as long as no one questioned him. they were uneasy about it but decided to follow him.

They follow Mal to where they needed to go and started recognizing the trees and where they were. So, they do apologize to the old man and start to trust him a little. They stop to make camp again and they start to notice someone is following them. Alessia and Neville start to think that their journey is not a secret anymore considering them seems to be other people that know of them traveling. Mal tells them, *"We are being tailed by a Naga warrior. There is no way to shake a warrior of that caliber easily. So, we must hope that he is an ally and we have nothing to worry about."* Alessia and Neville thought that the Naga race was extinct along with the old ways. This makes Mal laugh because hope never dies no matter what someone does to it.

Mal also says, *"This warrior is following you all because he is to protect someone in your group. I wonder who he could be following?"* he says as he looks at Sebak. Sebak was confused because he has never seen a Naga in his life. They travel further from that dirty town and for the night stops and make camp again. They still did not trust Mal fully but Sebak was starting to get curious why a Naga would be following him. But it was a matter they would have to learn about later. Keeping their eyes on what was in front of them but not forgetting about what was behind them.

They travel into a town that had soldiers ransacking the homes of innocent people looking for Sebak. News apparently travelled past them as they were travelling and Mal managed to keep them off of the main road for many moons. This town was a major town they had to pass through. It was the town of Natius, a battle torn town that has seen many wars. It barely recovered from any of them. Chaos ruled this town just like the last one they were in days ago. They cover Sebak up to get past the soldiers without any trouble. It worked for the ones at the entrance of the town. It was when they were trying to leave town were the problem arrived.

They did their best to sneak past the guards until they had nowhere else to go. They were stuck at the exit of the town with the sheriff and his men guarding it and checking people. When the guards approached them, Neville tried to talk their way past them. But there was too many of them paying attention. Hoping that they did not know who Sebak was they tried to say that he was a brother and gave him another name. The soldiers still did not fully believe their story until Mal enchanted him to let them pass. That surprised them all because magic is illegal inside of town. Mal says to them, "Only if you get caught." And he snickers a little. They manage to pass the guards and the Sheriff recognizes that they did not do what the other civilians were doing. The Sheriff walks towards then thinking they were hiding something from them.

Sebak knew it was over for them because he knew the sheriff's face. He had watched him fight before in the pits. He tells the rest of them this as the sheriff approached them. As he got closer, he started to recognize Sebak's face and was about to say as much. But Neville punches him in the face and everyone uncovers their weapons. Sebak was no help because he did not have weapon because he just escaped the colosseum a few days ago. Alessia, Neville, & Mal surround Sebak to protect him. the soldiers swarm them because they knocked the sheriff out. Neville and Alessia were the first two engaged when the fighting started. Mal used his walking stick against those that attacked him.

After a few attacks Mal he opens his walking stick to reveal a blade is on the end of his stick. The weapon was a Guandao (a long wooden polearm with a heavy curved blade at the end), not many people have been known to master such a weapon. To see one being used was very rare in their part of the world. To be able to hide it from people and disguise it as a walking stick was clever. Everyone engages someone to protect themselves. Sebak was forced to fight without a weapon. Before it got really serious with him a warrior dropped next to Sebak. He surprised everyone because they did not know where he came from.

The warrior gives Sebak a sword sheathed in its respected sheath. It was a curved hilted scimitar that Sebak likes to use. Not thinking about it he draws the weapon and feels the balance on the blade. He was in awe by the perfect balance of it. But begins to fight with it alongside this stranger. This warrior stepped out of the shadows revealing that he was the Naga warrior that was following them. Not many of the soldiers were killed in the fight, but many were injured. They ran in fear because they had not seen a Naga warrior before in this town. The group takes this chance to leave the town in their tracks as they mount their horses.

Once the fight was over the Naga shows himself to them. The warrior bows to the Sebak. Everyone was very confused because Sebak is not royalty. The warrior introduces himself as Scar a warrior of the Nagas. *"I do apologize if I have scared you or your companions. But I promised your real father that I would look out for you when you were born."* Sebak gets annoyed and starts to walk away because he wants nothing to do with his father because he never came to see him. Scar stands back up and tells him, *"He died before he could see you. He was a great warrior that did everything for your survival."* Sebak stops in his tracks to listen to Scar. *"He sacrificed his life so you could live. The humans did not understand him like I did. They call him a dark lord because he killed many humans. But he did so to protect our people and the world from a darkness that still was release. He failed to protect the world but your mother and him did not fail to protect you."*

Sebak looks down at the ground then looks back up at him to ask about his mother. Scar then bites his tongue (figuratively) because he did not want to mention the traitor. *"But the story of your mother is a difficult one to tell you. It's no easy way to say this young one but your parents had a major role in what has happened in the past. Not much of it is good. But they did what they could with what they were given."* Scar says. Neville and Alessia were surprised because Mal was correct. As for the blade Sebak attempts to give it back to Scar and tells him thank you. Scar tells him, *"I had it made in our people's forge. The blade will never break under any circumstances. The hilt is a symbol of our people and it will never fail you. If you know your way around a blade this weapon cannot fail. Sense you have drawn it for its first battle you must name it. This is the way of the Naga."* Sebak looks at the blade and thinks for a while. Even while they were traveling, he could not think of a name for the blade. Scar tells him, *"The name will come once you find yourself."*

The next day, they wake to a beautiful sunrise and they continue their journey towards Alessia and Neville's people. While the group was traveling Alessia noticed how beautiful the nature was and how it was untouched by anything. It surprised her because closer to the towns and the big castles the trees did not look this healthy. *"It was almost like being back home with my family and friends. Before the chaos took hold of our land that we had to run from. The elf that saved us told our parents that they would have a crucial part to play in the future. I still to this day do not understand why the elves took interest in us all those years ago."* she thinks to herself. Slowly the peace around them made her begin to sing her mother's favorite song in her head.

While they were camped Alessia beings to singing to the trees and the birds aloud. She does this as she is sitting alone on a rock watching nature. Little did she know Sebak could hear her singing. Once she realizes this she stops singing. Sebak steps up to her and tries to get her to sing once more. He told her, "I will leave I just wanted to know where that beautiful sound was coming from." As he does walk away. Obviously, she was shy about her singing and the only other person that knows of her singing is her mother. She watches as he departs from the area and she turns her head back towards the birds and begins to sing again but quieter so the others could not hear her.

Meanwhile, that night Sebak's sadness kicked in and he began to cry while he was trying to sleep. He did not bother anyone and kept it to himself and suffered in silence. He did not want to bother the others with his problems. Even when it was his turn to keep watch the sadness would sneak up on him. but he would not say anything to anyone and from that night forward it would attack him every night. The only one to notice that Sebak was in distress was Alessia. She did not know what to do about it until one day she confronted him about it.

One night both Alessia and Sebak spent the night talking about their past. Alessia would start by telling him about all the times she got into trouble with her brother Neville when they were children. The two of them were young and they decided to play with the village cook and mess with his food. They ended up doing chores for the cook for a week. But to Alessia the little bit of fun they had was worth the chores. Sebak would tell Alessia about the time he and his step father went to a lake on his birthday. He gave his step father a heart attack when he jumped off of a tall tree into the lake. His step father thought Sebak drowned in the lake. Both of them laughed as they reminisced about their childhood.

The night was beautiful and they could see every star in the sky. The crickets were chirping along with the frogs. Sebak was taking the watch closer to the morning so they were lucky to get to see the sun rise this night. While everyone was still sleeping and the sun was rising Alessia sums up the courage to sing next to Sebak. He was surprised because she did not like having an audience while she sang. Not to ruin the mood Sebak says quiet and just listens to her sing not wanting to interrupt her. He could not help but look her in the eye while she sang and he started to notice a lot of things about her. Because of this Alessia stops singing and goes to pack her things. As she walks away Sebak tells her, *"Thank you. That was beautiful my friend."*

The next day, they continue their journey through the woods with ease. until the woods ended abruptly because it has been burned because of towns being burned to the ground because of the rebellion. The sight was very sad and gruesome, many bodies lay burned all over the burning woods. Some animals perished during the huge fire apparently and it saddened Alessia and Sebak. Neville and Mal did not show any emotion towards the sight they were seeing. It was just a shame to see so much death for nothing but chaos.

CHAPTER 4: SHATTERED

The group had to go through the town now that they were out in the open without any cover. Scar scouted ahead to figure out how this happened in the first place. Alessia and Neville were on edge because they have seen this work once before. Mal could feel the presence of four other beings but he could not pinpoint were. As they walked further into the town of ashes everyone was more on edge. It was only once they were in the center of the town that Mal could tell what they were dealing with. But it was too late for him to warn anyone in the group. As he begins to warn Sebak and the others a warriors jump out from the ashes to jump Alessia, Neville, & Sebak. Scar intercepts the one that had the jump on Sebak just narrowly by pulling Sebak out of the way.

One engages Alessia and Neville at the same time knocking them off balance. A third warrior engages Sebak from behind him. The fourth assailant attacks Mal to keep him from assisting anyone. These warriors were well trained in the ways of separating their opponents. The warrior fighting Alessia and Neville knew how to break them down and he did it quickly. The one fighting Scar had trouble because he had never encountered a Naga before now. Mal's opponent could sense who he was and it was throwing him off balance a little. Sebak's opponent knew how to get into the young man's head.

The warrior fighting Mal was putting up a good fight but realized he was terribly outmatched by Mal. He could not help but wonder why his opponent was playing with him. using his abilities, he fully learned who Mal was and he decided to cut and run. Once Mal realized what the warrior knew he had to kill him on the spot to protect his secret. As the warrior was trying to escape Mal uses telekinesis to stop the warrior in his tracks and choke him to death with it. Mal could feel his grip slipping and decides to throw his weapon and decapitate him.

Alessia and Neville were struggling to fight their opponent because their opponent was a rival of Neville's. This man was one of the warriors that helped burn their homes and slaughter many of their innocent people. This was an emotional battle for the two of them. But their opponent just played with them. Even though they had the number advantage against their opponent he was prepared to destroy them mentally and physically. During their engagement the warrior disables Neville by nicking his right arm and his left leg. Making Neville fall to the ground defenseless. Alessia jumps to her brother's defense intercepting what could have been a killing blow.

Scar and his opponent were almost completely even in their style of sword form. The warrior began to get arrogant about the situation and thought the old man was getting slow. This was not the case at all for Scar. He was studying his opponent as their fight escalated. The warrior did not realize this until it was almost too late. Once Scar started to slowly get the upper hand the warrior broke of the fight. He retreats to their group leader as he also was leaving the fight. This annoys Scar until he thinks about Sebak and runs towards his location. Moving as quickly as he could hoping he did not fail Bakari in the slightest.

Sebak and his opponent were almost not fighting because he was playing with his food. The warrior was completely playing with Sebak in almost every way. Once he was inside Sebak's head mentally the fight was almost too easy. At first, he was putting up a good fight against the unknown warrior. But he figured out how to break the young warrior. Once the warrior felt his comrade fall, he decided to retreat from the fight. As he also heard feet coming into his direction. As he was leaving Scar appeared and engaged him for half a second as the warrior was attempting to escape. Sebak was beside himself because of all his trauma came flooding into his mind. His hands began to shake from all the sadness he was holding back.

Mal arrives to see Alessia holding Neville because of his injuries. Neville began to crack jokes as the cuts were not deep enough to kill him but they were deep enough to leave a scar. He says, "It took years to obtain a perfect body like mine and that sow decided to mark up my beautiful body." Alessia rolls her eyes at her brother's comment. Mal walks over and touches Neville's forehead to heal him. the cuts go away in the matter of seconds and it was like nothing ever happened. Neville jumps up and hugs Mal and tells him thank you. Alessia tells Mal thank you as well for helping her brother.

They go to check on Sebak and Scar and they discover an almost mentally broken Sebak. He was on his knees shaking because of what the warrior said to him and what he could hear in his head. Mal had to tell Sebak that they were Psi Warriors and they seem to have been trained to hunt and break an opponent mentally before killing them. But Sebak wasn't hearing it from Mal because he felt like everyone around him was lying to him. Because the psi warrior also learned something the others did not know about Sebak.

While Sebak walks away to find peace in his mind once more, Scar was also in shock a little. Scar tells the rest of them that Sebak isn't just an ordinary Naga. The young lad is the last of his kind being a Dragiir Naga.

Just like the Dragiir changeling they were very rare in these dark times because of the prophecy that was foretold centuries ago. A Dragiir version of their race is the most powerful of their races. Long ago created by the great dragon Phyrra assisted by the wizard Elurian. The magic of a Dragiir is almost living and its very potent to anything evil. Believed to be decedents of dragons themselves. But no one could ever prove it because there has only ever been two in history. Sebak makes the third Dragiir to ever walk the world of Navaria. A Dragiir is believed to have limitless magic if trained correctly and if they have full control of themselves. Something Bakari almost achieved in his lifetime. But destroyed himself because he absorbed souls.

But Sebak was different because he did not have the training mentally to keep the psi warriors out of his mind. Everyone regroups and high tails it out of the area so they could not be attacked again. They began to move quicker than they usually were during the day and Mal was covering their tracks. Alessia was worried about Sebak because he did not seem to be recovering from what the psi warrior had done to him. they couldn't help him in any way he would have to sort it out for himself. Even Mal was beginning to worry about Sebak himself. He had to do something that would help the young lad see the light.

One day before they decided to move from their camp Mal pushes Sebak into an area for them to train. Sebak got angry at Mal for pushing him and tells him, "This is for your own good. This is to break your mind free from that trauma. I know you are stronger than this Sebak. Stop wallowing in your self-pity." He draws his weapon against Sebak and attacks him. Sebak draws his sword only to protect himself. Mal swings wildly at Sebak to get him to fight back. He did not want to fight his friend and his resolve was breaking. Because of this Sebak's blade shatters as Mal hits the blade. The only one not shocked was Scar about the blade breaking. Sebak takes the hilt of the sword and runs away from his friends. Alessia and Neville began to question Scar on why the blade shattered the way it did. He tells them, *"The blade has bonded with its master. If its master is shattered then the blade will shatter. It's up to Sebak to find himself in this world. Once he does that the blade will come back to protect him. Our weapons are for warriors and the blade cannot faulter. We use a unique magic to keep our blades sharp. We have to be bonded to our weapon and it can assist us in battle. Once the blade and its master are on the same page, they can be unstoppable. Maybe now Sebak will learn the name of his blade during this time."* He says as Alessia goes to check on Sebak and leaves Neville with Mal and Scar. She did not want him to be alone while he was so vulnerable.

Meanwhile, the Psi warriors regroup with only the three of them in the woods. Together they meet their leader in the shadows. He was not pleased with their failure and the fact they lost one of their own. It was Warden Sir. Fulchard himself one of the men that did not like Sir Edger and his family. Meaning the Psi warriors had their eyes on them for the longest. Only because they thought they could possibly turn Sebak to their side at some point. Now they think he is too far gone. Their master

Prince Kaein gave them orders that if they could not turn Sebak to the side of chaos then they should eliminate him. this time sir Fulchard and his right-hand Psi warrior would join them in the next attack. Deciding to wait for the perfect time to strike the so-called heroes.

Sebak was beside himself and didn't know what to do because his step father expected so much of him. but he does not know life outside of the gladiator colosseum. This is the first time in a long time he has been able to see the world. Alessia joins him while he sits watching nature alone. She decides to talk him down and out of this mental hole he was in. she tells him, *"You must beat this Sebak your parents know you are strong. Even I have come to think you are as well. You have become a good friend to me Sebak I do not open up to anyone. But your presence is soothing enough for me to feel able to talk to you. Was I wrong to trust you?"* Sebak answers her question with a firm, *"No you were not. But..."* she cuts him off before he could finish his sentence. The word but is for anyone that is about to make an excuse. You do not make excuses my friend you are strong on the inside I have seen it. As I have seen how cute you can be when you're trying." She laughs as she finishes the sentence. Which makes Sebak laugh and he begins to hug her. This action surprises her because she was not expecting a hug. He tells her, *"Thank you. I need that Alessia. You are a very special person and I will protect that kindness because there is not much of that in this world anymore."* Once they were finished hugging Neville joins them.

Neville catches his sister blushing because of Sebak's word and he starts to mess with her ruining the moment as she chases him away. Making Sebak laugh at the two of them because he never knew what it was like having a sibling. He grew up alone and then in a cage with people that wanted to kill him. Once Sebak felt better he and Mal went back to training to get Sebak's confidence back up. So, they used staffs for the time being until they were comfortable with using blades. Scar decided that he would teach Neville and Alessia a trick that the Naga and a few other races use when they are in a fight.

Weeks pass as they are traveling and there was no sign of the warriors that were hunting them. That seemed very suspicious in a way to Scar and Mal because why attack someone and mentally destroy their opponent and then vanish. This tactic had no logic behind it that they could see but they kept their eyes open for anything suspicious. Alessia and Neville were also worried about the people hunting them. But they did not show it on their faces because they were trying to keep Sebak's mind off of the events going on around him. Mal had to snap Sebak back into reality every time they trained so the lad could learn to focus once again. While Scar was training Alessia and Neville he wanted to know why that warrior was so frightening to them. They dismissed that they were ever frightened of the man they faced until Scar gave them a stern look. They caved and then told Scar about how he was a part of the massacre of their village once. Scar did not expect this to come out of their mouths. The man they fought burned down their home and marked Alessia. He marked her in a way that he would always know where she is. So once his service is done, he could either kill her or marry her. Scar realized this is why the hunters were not attacking. It was because one of them could track them.

Scar goes and tells Mal of the situation that they were dealing with. The news even surprised Sebak a little and it angered him in a way. But he did not want to show his anger because he did not want to show his feelings about Alessia. Mal decided to set off a trap for their hunters because they will eventually come for them. They could not lead them back to their people Alessia thought so they needed to fight them and get rid of them. But she did not tell everyone the truth about the entire situation. She feared that they would get rid of her. So, she kept the full truth to herself. Even though she knows secrets can destroy anything if it's a strong enough lie.

They picked their place for the trap on a mountain far away from the roads and away from a secret that Mal and Scar knew about. The two of them were leading the young ones to a secret island that no one knows of but the heroes of the past. Heroes that are still alive and still opposing the chaos. This island they were leading the young ones to was called Themyscira. An island that has managed to stay hidden from humanity for centuries until a young woman found it and created a civilization on it. The island was originally hidden by the elf named Elurian centuries ago to be his ark to save races from the old world.

During this down time, Neville and Sebak made a friendly banter on who could shoot the best. Neville was more of a spear thrower while Sebak was an archer. While they were waiting and making tracks to their camp on purpose Neville won three games before Sebak could get on the board. Then they went another five rounds and Neville was up to five wins and Sebak was up to four wins before that night. Sebak told Neville that he was just lucky because he did not fully master archery. The two of them laughed it off in the long run. Mal and Scar could see a strong bond between the three of them. "One like the Shield brothers had before the end of their story." Mal says to Scar. Scar was confused because he never saw him during those years.

Scar was very confused for few seconds until Mal answers his question. Mal tells him, *"I was watching the entire time. I could not help or do anything because of my injuries. I still bare some injuries and cannot over exert myself too much. I believe I will one day die of these injuries but not before I do some good in this world. I have caused too much pain in this world and I want to reverse it."* Scar understood that because he has heard something similar of those lines from his old friend Bakari. Scar says to Mal, *"You have to tell them the truth my friend. If you do not someone else will and it could break you all apart and make them question everything. To keep them as a stronger unit they must know they can trust their mentors. Something the shield brothers did not have when they were coming up. They were destroyed from the inside. Give these young ones a chance at hope of destroying the chaos."*

Mal sits and thinks about this most of his watch at night. Even during the day when they are all interacting with one another. He looks at them then looks down at the ground to avoid eye contact. Knowing what he must do he had to sit down and talk to them all once this was all over. Even going as far as telling the three of them that he has a secret he must tell them one day. But it would not be smart to tell them now because of the circumstances they are in at the moment. But he promises that he would tell them once they reached their destination. Alessia, Neville, & Sebak agree to hear him out once this is all said and done.

Scar says to Mal, *"That is one way of saving it. But now you have to own up to it. This is only the beginning of your redemption my friend. This is just the start and we will be with you for the rest of the way. But if your redemption is merely a game, I will not hesitate to hunt you down and destroy you."* Mal reassures him, *"This is no game I have seen the evil I have brought into this world and I regret all of it. Even the pain I have caused my only friend in the world when I was in my youth. I now have something to fight for."* As Mal looks at Sebak.

CHAPTER 5: SERENITY

While the group was fishing for food Neville and Alessia had a moment to talk to one another. Neville could see his sister smiling again this made him happy that they took the job to rescue Sebak. Because he has not seen his sister smile for over five or more years now. He has seen her fake smile and half smile. In his world he does not count either of those as a real smile. Neville always worries about his sister even if she does not want him to. Because that is the duty of a big brother is to protect his little sister from harm. Feeling like he has failed her for the past five or more years after the burning of their camp with their family.

Seeing that Psi warrior again that was cruel to their people and helped slaughter many innocent people brought back many memories. But for Alessia the time of their journey and spending time with the people around them has made her smile once again. It seems to have given her purpose on this earth. Beforehand she was often brooding a lot and would often lash out at people. As she aged, she has gotten more in control than she used to be. Just like Sebak she would often suffer in silence. Neville would be the only person to calm her down until she seemed to have met someone, she can open up to other than her brother. The two siblings talk about it without anyone else around. because Alessia is afraid to lose a potential good friend.

Neville tells his little sister, *"You don't know what could happen sis. You must give him a chance and yourself one. Life is not easy and it will always bring a new obstacle in your path. If you find someone that is with you to the end that is a beautiful thing. If it's just as friends that is okay too. Because of what happened in the past you cannot think everyone is the same. You must keep getting back up sis. I'm here for you no matter what and for every decision you make. As long as you are breathing sis you are here for a reason and pain is not the reason. You are here to do something in this world. You must figure out what it is on your own."*

During the time the siblings were having a moment and Neville was motivating his sister they were attacked. The Psi warriors returned to finish the job and this time everyone was separated already. The perfect time to attack their opponents was when they least expect it. This time their leader Sir Fulchard was with them and he engaged Mal and Scar at the same time to keep them away from the young ones. Alessia and Neville ended up fighting the same man that wants Alessia to join them or perish. They were engaged in two verses two because this time the warrior had support. Sebak was facing the same man that destroyed his courage a few weeks ago. The warrior could sense something different about Sebak but he could not put his finger on it.

Warden Sir Fulchard was able to keep the two mentors at bay with ease because Mal was unable to put full effort into the fight. He could only defend himself realizing that he has put too much magic and energy into training Sebak. Scar on the other hand was worried about Mal and would not full-on attack and leave Mal open. Mal knew that he was the weak link in this bought. He had to figure out how to get out of the fight without leaving himself open to attack and protect Scar as well. The fight was completely a stalemate and that is how Sir Fulchard wanted it. He taunted them as much as possible to attack so they would forget about the young ones. He prayed on Scar's pride of a duel and knew he would not cut and run unless it was an emergency or his opponent stops the fight.

Alessia and Neville were almost completely expecting the attack to come at this moment. They drew their weapons and stood back-to-back ready to engage their opponents. Neville with his javelins protecting himself and his sister. Alessia with her bow and arrows ready to shoot anyone that made a move. The warriors did not outright engage them yet but taunted them because of the stance they were in. the formation that the siblings wherein did not have an opening and anyone who attacked would be hit with something. they had to play this smart.

Sebak on the other hand was standing face to face with his opponent with his hilt in his hand. The psi warrior thought this was a joke because he was unarmed and threatened him with a hilt. He laughed at Sebak and asked him, *"This is how you want to die?"* as he readies his halberd. Sebak was inside his mind and ignored his opponent and was trying to find his peace. He was meditating in front of him and left himself open intentionally. *"All the training we have endured was meant for this. I must not break down again because life will try to break me every day I wake up. This is where I make my stand and I will no longer be a pawn in my own story. I must find serenity"* He thinks to himself. The warrior charges him while his eyes are closed.

Sebak just moves on instinct and put the hilt in front of the attack and his sword's blade returned to protect him. he parries the warrior and then looks at the hilt and called it, *"Serenity. This will be your name."* he says in his head. This fight was very different from the first time they battled. They two fought as if they have trained together. Sebak seemed to be on another level now. It almost seemed as it Sebak was now playing with him. it started to aggravate his assailant. But Sebak could read all of his movements thanks to Mal and Scar's training. He wasn't getting arrogant but he was very proud of himself as they battled. While his opponent was not happy with what was happening.

Meanwhile, Alessia and Neville where still in their formation and their opponents were trying to bargain with them. But Neville would never give up his sister because it's his duty as a brother to protect her from evil like them. So, the warriors support attempts to attack the formation and Neville moves to engage him. but Alessia's hunter psionic blasts the both of them and his own partner. Knocking the two of them down and his ally recovered at the last second. The hunter reveals his real name was Boulevard and he wanted what he came for even if he had to kill it. Boulevard used a fake name when he was attempting to destroy their home camp.

Alessia tried to fight him with her bow and arrows to no avail. He was prepared for her ranged attacks. So, she had to fight him with her daggers against his longsword. Boulevard did nothing but play with Alessia until her brother attempted to attack him. but his ally intercepted Neville. The four of them fought like everything depended on it. Alessia was holding her own against Boulevard for a while. It was this way until he started to get annoyed with her acrobatics. So, he goes and catches her left arm when she goes to block him. Boulevard proceeds to knee her in the gut causing her to drop her weapons. She ends up falling to her knees leaving herself wide open for a killing blow. Boulevard goes for a downward slash that would be a killing blow on a defenseless Alessia.

Neville in one fluid motion blocks his opponent and then maneuvers to throw his javelin at Boulevard to knock him off balance. Leaving himself unarmed for only a second because when the javelin hits Boulevard it knocks him off his attack on Alessia. The weapon then proceeds to return to its owner after breaking up the attack from Boulevard. Neville catches the javelin before his opponent could attack him. Alessia jumps from one knee and spin kicks Boulevard in the face before he could recover from the surprise attack Neville did. These moves shocked Boulevard as he sees they have become a more effective unit than they use to be all those years ago.

Mal and Scar manage to hold their own against Sir Fulchard. Until they realized what the enemy's plan was. Their full plan was to divide them all completely and destroy them. Meaning that Mal could not leave Scar to fight Sir Fulchard because he would kill him or attempt to. From what Mal was sensing the young ones need this moment to grow. And these hunters have provided the perfect chance for them to adapt and grow or they will die. This was a chance they had to take. Because no hero is created with ease.

Mal and Scar figure out their own balance in fighting Sir Fulchard. They had to make their weaknesses their strength. The two of them would have to protect one another in this fight. Sir Fulchard could sense they were about to get serious in their fight now because they were not worried about the young ones. Mal had to fight though the pain but he was hiding where it was from Sir Fulchard. In the blink of an eye the three of them seemed to fight faster than the speed of light. Anyone watching that was not trained in the ways of the sword could not keep up with their speed. Scar and Mal covered each other as best they could against Sir Fulchard. The entire time Mal thinks about how evil has grown over the centuries because of him. Then Sir Fulchard felt a disturbance and he cut the fight and retreated.

Sebak's opponent now feared him because of what he was seeing from him. the young man's eyes were in their final stage. His eyes where now slit like snake eyes and it did nothing but stuck fear into the heart of his opponent causing him to slip up while they were battling. Giving Sebak the chance for a killing blow in the stomach. Once his opponent was down his eyes went back to normal. He quickly thought of Alessia and Neville and rushed to their aid as fast as he could. Thinking to himself, "I will not lose my friends to this evil. I have faith that they will win the day. I will not let my friends fall on this day." As he runs up the mountain to them.

Neville and his opponent moved up the mountain along with Alessia and Boulevard. But Neville's opponent was trying his best to keep him away from Boulevard and Alessia. She was struggling against Boulevard a little but she was also holding her own. Neville wanted to help his sister badly because this would not be like it was when their family was in danger. Neville manages to get the drop on his opponent and backstab him with the javelin. After he pulls it from his opponent's side Sir Fulchard arrives and knocks Neville off of his feet. He flies into a tree and is knocked senseless. But he still tries to stand because of his adrenaline to protect his sister.

Mal and Scar could sense what was happening and was trying to get there as fast as they could. Mal being in pain he was moving slowly and Scar could only move fast when he was fighting. Sir Fulchard wanted this to be over because they were losing too many men for this one woman that his apprentice was obsessed with. Sir Fulchard tells Neville, "Stay down son. You do not want to die here." Neville couldn't speak because of the damage he just received. All he could do was stand up and hold his weapon. He tried to walk towards Sir Fulchard but to no avail. Neville dropped after taking two steps and passed out. Sir Fulchard smirked because it was funny how people try so hard and then fail.

Boulevard and Alessia were on the cliff fighting and he was getting angry fighting her. He finally managed to knock all of her weapons out of her hand. She still would not give up the fight. She would not accept Boulevard as a lover or anything of that nature. Alessia only saw him as the man that tried to kill her family. Forever in her mind he would be a scoundrel that she wanted dead. This angered Boulevard enough to knock her down in the position for him to slice her head off. He really did not want to kill her but she was not giving him a choice. He goes for the killing blow once again on Alessia.

Sebak appears in front of Alessia and catches Boulevard's blade. Instinctively somehow Sebak used an ability called, "The flash step". This ability allows for the user to teleport to their ally. Mal and Scar could see them from down below and Mal stopped Scar to see what was about to happen. Scar wanted to help the young ones but Mal told him not yet let's see what happens. Scar didn't understand why Mal was playing with their lives. But he could see the conviction in Mal's face as well. They wanted to know what the young ones were capable of. Their training was to prepare them to face their past. But Sebak had never faced Sir Fulchard before in a duel. But he has been a man that has spoken out against Sebak in the past.

Sir Fulchard could sense why those soldiers were afraid of Sebak all those years ago. Seeing the lad had snake eyes he jumps to help Boulevard. Sebak pushes Boulevard back and Fulchard attacks Sebak. But he was quick enough to block his attack with Serenity. Sebak was calm and collected when engaging Sir Fulchard. The two began to duel and Sebak seemed to be more superior with a blade than Sir Fulchard was. This feat annoyed Sir Fulchard a lot so he asked for his apprentice's help. When Boulevard tried to get up and get into the fight Sebak used magical lightening on Boulevard to shock him and keep him down. Keeping the fight one on one. Sebak was even using one arm to combat Sir Fulchard's strikes.

Seeing how well put Sebak was Sir Fulchard decides to retreat from the fight. He backs off and takes Boulevard with him. He tells Sebak that they would meet again and Sebak response was that he hopes so. Once they were gone, he checks on Alessia to see if she was okay. She was shaking but ultimately fine physically. But Neville was not okay physically. He was injured more than Mal could fix on his own. They needed to get him to a place that he could stay without being moved a lot. Mal tells them that he knows of a place. But it was still a little way away for them. Only because they would have to cross the ocean to get to their destination. It was the only place they could be safe for a while without anyone attacking them.

Sebak and Alessia make a sled for them to carry Neville on and they tie him down on it. They continue their travels hoping that they make it to their destination. It took a while for them to make it to the beach because they were worried about Neville's health. Which they should have been he had broken ribs and many lacerations on his body. In the wilderness it could do nothing but get infected. Mal did not know enough healing magic to help him completely. He could only do small cuts or something of that nature. This was far more extensive than he could heal.

Once they made it to the harbor of Natius they commandeered a ship so they could go to their mystery island. They did not have enough money to actually buy a ship so Scar and Sebak used their eyes to hypnotize someone into giving their ship away. The group left as quickly as possible before the person realized what has happened. Scar realizing that Sebak has full control over his Naga abilities meant he was coming of age in their heritage. It was time for him to make a bond with an animal of his choosing. This is something he would have to teach him about considering Bakari isn't alive to show him and Sebak's mother is not here to show him either. But before doing so he would have to teach him more about his heritage.

They drifted on the ocean for hours before Alessia started to get restless for her brother. Because Neville need help now and they were not going to get it in the middle of the ocean. But Mal proved her wrong because they happened to pass through a barrier as she was beginning to yell at Mal. They discover a beautiful island untouched by chaos and war. And it surprised them all except Mal because he was the only one that knew it was there. He only knew this because in his youth this was once his home. Their ship hits the coast and Mal tells everyone to put their weapons down.

They all were confused because they didn't see anyone. Mal urges them to put their weapons down even the Naga hilts because these people could sense magic.

They put their weapons down with no argument and many warriors appeared around them from using invisibility magic. These warriors were all female and they all had bows on them. From what Mal says, *"These warriors have been watching us from the moment we came through the barrier. We must be cautious in what we do or they will not help us."* Alessia was not happy with this but anything to help her brother. More women arrive to meet them on the coast. It seemed to be their Queen that meets them at the edge of their barrier. Mal tells them to kneel before the queen of Themyscira.

CHAPTER 6: THE AMAZONS

The Queen of Themyscira was named, "Tessa Eskilsson" a name that Scar recognized well. She bared the last name of a warrior that valiantly fought against Aethos when he was released. He was the first of many to fall by the hands of the Chaos Titan. He met her father Bjor before the Chaos Titan was released into the world. He was a good man with a strong daughter then. She has grown and started her own community away from the world. A community made of nothing but women. Here in Themyscira the women find power within themselves. Mal had no choice but to bring his companions here even though he never officially met anyone on Themyscira. He only knew that this island once was his home when he was young and the plants here could help Neville.

The women on the island did not appreciate having four males on their island. They did not want to hear anything from the males but why they were here. Queen Tessa says, *"Why are you here and I do not want to hear any of your male lies."* Alessia had to speak for them and tell the Amazonians, *"We are only here to save her brother Neville. I do not know how Mal knew of this place. But he said it would help and I trust him."* The queen wanted to know how did they know of the island. Mal tells them, *"I knew of it because it was once my home before you all moved into it."* This comment confuses them because when they inhabited the island there was no sign of anyone ever living here. But it did not confuse Tessa completely because of the history she learned from her father. But the people before them were elves and no one among them were elves. At least not that they could see with their eyes. Until she looked at Mal and realized he was using strong magic to keep up his disguise. The Queen says, *"Let them in and help the wounded one. But keep your eyes on this Mal."* She says as she stares him down.

Knowing who Scar was Queen Tessa tells the soldiers, *"Scar is free to walk the grounds of this castle. He might meet someone that he once knew."* She says with a smirk. They pick Neville up on a sled to transport him to the castle. Sebak was to stay next to Scar because they could tell Scar was his mentor. The two of them could train as long as they needed to while they were there. As for Alessia they could tell she has suffered from a traumatic experience. The Queen tells her, *"We can help you find your true inner warrior my daughter."* Alessia looks at her and says, *"With all due respect your highness I am not your daughter. How do you know I need help?"* Tessa says, *"Because many come in here shaking for some reason. They find their place here or they take their training and make a better life for themselves somewhere else. We are only here to empower women because we too have a voice in this world."*

Alessia recognized that saying because her mother use to say, *"Every woman has a voice. It's up to you to make others here it."* She was beginning to understand where her mother's training came from. Tessa was happy for this news because they don't get many second-generation warriors here. The two of them walk the castle grounds watching women training getting ready for something. they all worked together like a huge family. The place was beautiful and well put together. She asks Tessa, *"what are you getting ready*

for?" Tessa answers, *"We are getting ready for something my father was preparing me for... Ragnarök. The ending battle that would end time for us as we know it. At least that is how my father would put it. I believe there is more to it though. So, we prepare for the arrival of the great war."*
They walk to where Neville was being held and Alessia thanks Tessa for her hospitality. Tessa was happy should help a family once again get back on their feet. She leaves them to talk and reminisce about their old days. Tessa goes to find Mal and to speak to him alone without anyone else in ear shot of them.

Tessa was curious what Mal was because there were not many beings that know of Themyscira. Only the elves knew of this place centuries before they left. This island has been able to be untouched by chaos and evil itself. It would be annoying to allow it to walk right through the front door in disguise. She walks up with soldiers and finds him using magic in his room to heal himself. That was not all he was doing in there. He seemed to have gathered herbs from their land to help him heal himself. Looking at it through the door the wound was not physical it was some sort of magical wound. The decides to give him some respect and knocks on his door. He tells her to come in because he already knew she was there.

Mal knew his secret was not safe here. So, he tells her, *"I know you do not know me. I can understand your caution. I would be the same way if a stranger appeared on my border and was hiding his identity. But you do not get to know before my apprentice and his friend does. I do not want them to learn who I am from anyone else but me. I promise you I will answer all your questions once they learn the truth and decide if they still want me as a mentor. All you need to know is I am on the side of life. I have no other agendas but to keep Sebak alive."* Tessa looked him in the eye the entire time which made her believe everything he said because a lying person would not be able to look her in the eye.

She tells him, *"Okay old man I give you two hours to tell your companions who you are. Then you will have to tell me everything you know. I would love to know how this was once your home. Cross me before then and I will kill you myself sorcerer."* She says she walks away. Assuming that he is one seeing the magic he was using to heal himself. He was only attempting to heal himself because he knows he is living on borrowed time. The healing magic is only temporary because the spell that injured him is permanent. No one can undo the spell not even the person that put it on him. even though the spell was aimed at a friend and he protected them.

Mal sits in the room for a while thinking about what happened all those years ago. How he was in the wrong and his best friend paid the ultimate price for his stupid mistakes. Being blinded by his own ambition and did not realize he was being used for real evil to arise and take his place. He has caused the world real harm and he did not want anyone to know who he really was. He can feel all the pain he has caused because of what he has done. The injury that is killing him helps him feel empathy for the ones he has wronged. He was misguided because of what has happened to him as a child. But one person was always his friend even when they were fighting one another. He thinks, *"This is how I get redemption... helping Sebak and his friends save the world. I don't care if I go to hell as long as I have helped in some way and protect this world from being covered in Chaos. I was wrong to do what I have done. I do not deserve forgiveness."*

Meanwhile, Scar and Sebak are taking in the beauty of the island. They did not want to worry about their friend Neville because he was in good hands. Scar had to get Sebak ready because he was ready for the right of passage in the way of the Naga. It was time for him to bond with a creature. to most it called taming a creature. but Nagas's bond with their pets for many reasons. For some they are granted their senses to use for everyday life and others they learn more from their bonding from the animal that makes them feel one with nature. Some Nagas even has the capability to transform into a snake. If they do not learn to make a bond with their pet then they will lose all of their abilities and become human.

Sebak didn't feel like it was so bad because his Naga heritage has done nothing but cause him to be hunted. Scar could tell he was just lashing out because he would not tell him of his mother. From what he did say she was not a good person to be around. So why learn of her heritage seeing how both his parents were apparently evil in many people's eyes. Then someone steps out of the shadows to disagree with the young Sebak.

The person that stepped out of the shadows was no one other than Nyssa a Naga Queen that was a changeling like Sebak's father Bakari. Her and Scar embrace one another and kiss each other. Because he did not know when he would see his wife again. Sebak felt awkward because they kissed in front of him without warning. But Nyssa was against everything that Sebak was saying. She says, *"Both of your parents have their flaws. Your father wanted what was good for you and so did your mother. They did not know how to go about doing it. Bakari didn't know you existed until he returned to this realm and took the throne from your mother. She sent you to the humans so none of the Chaos army could find you. As a baby you looked like the child of prophecy and she had to hide you. This was the only reason Bakari spared her life."*

Sebak was confused a little now because Scar said that his mother was evil. Nyssa agrees with what Sebak just said and tells him, *"Yes, she was very conniving and a backstabber. But she had a soft spot for her children. even though she had many of them because she was the Naga Queen. But she held you and one other close to her heart. Meaning she had favorites even though they say you shouldn't have favorites."* This made Sebak feel a little better about his mother. *"With all of her flaws she loves you Sebak more than she lets on. Even though the moment Bakari was killed she took the throne from me."* Nyssa informs them. Letting Sebak know that his mother is defiantly still alive.

"No young man you must learn how to make a bond like my husband said. Or you will lose half of your legacy and your father wouldn't want that." Nyssa says to Sebak. *"I have seen what you can do my apprentice and you are like your father. He was able to become a hex blade. But he barely scratched the surface. Without training he lost his chance to gain the skills. He became a soul dragon and became ticking time bomb instead. But you are nothing like that lad. You seem to be unique because you have more control over your anger."* Scar says to Sebak.

Tessa appears to see that Scar and Nyssa have found one another on their own. Another family she could help reunite once again after all this time. Upon arriving she could see Mal watching the three of them from afar and shaking. Because his time to tell them was running out on him. but she was not going to pressure him, she was going to let the pressure of time do that for her. She decided to wait and see what was going to happen with all of them. Going back to her throne room to deal with problems of her community. Which was never much to do considering they ran a strong community that did not have many issues.

Mal walks away to check on Neville before he begins telling them the truth. Because he did not know if they would accept him once the truth was free. Upon seeing Neville, he also ran into Alessia which did not leave his side the entire time they have been here. He was sleeping when Mal arrived. Alessia tells him this much and he still wanted to check on him because he felt like everything was about to change and he would not see him the same way. Alessia could not figure out why Mal was acting weird all of a sudden. But Mal dismissed what she said and tells her to meet him on the coast. There is where he will tell them all who he really is.

Alessia agrees to it and tells him that she will have to inform Neville after they talk because he may not be able to walk around by then. Mal goes back to Sebak and the rest to tell them the same thing. They all were very confused because he seemed very down about what he was about to say to them. But he says finish training Sebak first because it was more important that what he had to say. In reality he did not know if he would be around to see Sebak grow fully in his true potential. Because the news he had could cause him to be kicked out of the group and away from everyone. They could possibly execute him for what he has done in the past. So, he decides to sit and watch Sebak's greatness rise one last time he thought. The others thought he was acting weird for a man that barely knows them.

Scar and Nyssa were attempting to help Sebak unlock his true potential in the training field. Alessia comes out to see what was happening with them all. Seeing a woman next to Scar coaching Sebak. She could not help but get curious on what was happening. Tessa also showed up and thought that what was happening was weird. But she quickly picked up on what was happening and asked them if she could help Sebak focus. She brought in their sages to assist him in fully meditating properly. Usually, he could meditate without help but this was a different type of meditation. He had to go fully under and face himself. Once doing so he could be at peace on the inside of his soul.

Sebak goes into the meditation and finds himself. His dark self was very powerful because of his self-guilt. He was starting to struggle to even walk close to his dark self. The two had a conversation about the past and how he failed his step-father, mother, and his first mentor the monk. They all died because of him and is anger issues. The real Sebak did not know what to do because he knew that was true. It was his fault that his family is gone and his first mentor is gone. That was very true, but he could not let that own him is what he started to think about. But the dark side of him tells him, *"You will only get your new family killed. One of them is already dying and you don't even realize it."* This made Sebak concerned and it made him think who could it be. This gives the dark side of him a chance to attack him.

Everyone could see that Sebak was struggling with all his might against his darker self. Mal could not allow the guilt to get the lad killed in any way. So, without anyone paying attention to him Mal goes into a meditative sleep to jump into Sebak's mind. He sees that Sebak is fighting his darker self and he seemed to be losing the fight. Because it was a rite of passage he could not directly interfere with the fight. Sebak must do it alone in order to become a man in his people's eyes. But there was something else Mal could do for the young lad.

Mal decides to tell the truth that he was hiding from Sebak that was also hurting him not to tell Sebak. *"Son your stepfather did not die when you escaped. Actually, he never existed at all he was a character in my arsenal. It was me and it always has been. I cannot bring your mother back because she was the second person in this horrible world to ever show me kindness. I wish I could bring her back but I can't. As for the monk as well, he was nothing more than another character to play in your growth. I have been every voice that has ever whispered in your ear. I just could not tell you because you were young and needed a push in the right direction. I missed that chance with your father. So, I tried to make sure you went down the correct path that your father did not. I was lucky to end up adopting you as my own."*

"I understand if you don't believe me son. I wouldn't believe me at this moment. But there is something that only you and your step father know about. I use to tell you about Honor... what do you know about honor? You... who never faced true fear learn what honor is before pretending you

are a warrior. Know this… before you step on to that thin red path where no misstep is allowed. A path that only ends when your legs fail to support you and when your heart stops beating. A path where sadness goes along with pain and where glory is the color of blood. This narrow path goes only one way. A way covered with enemies and brothers and it will take you without any shame into the hands of death for the name you were given and for your descendants." Sebak was shocked by Mal's words and gets impowered by his words.

Because of what Mal told him the darker side of Sebak did not have anything to stand on. Sebak defeats his darker side being empowered by Mal's words of the truth. Once awakens he runs to Mal and hugs him because he always had a warm feeling towards Mal like he was like a father to him. Now he fully knew why he always felt that way towards Mal. Everyone else was confused on why Sebak jumped up and hugged Mal.

CHAPTER 7: THE TRUTH

Mal tells Sebak not to celebrate just yet because he could still hate him in the next few minutes after he tells the full truth. Sebak tells them that Mal was his step father when he was growing up. Mal shows them by changing into Sir Edger and shocking the rest of them. But he changes back into the old man because Sir Edger is dead to the world now. Also, because it took a lot to change like that. He only did it to show them that he could do that. This surprised everyone except Nyssa and Scar. But Scar already had his suspicions about him. they asked, *"So you're a changeling?"* Mal tells them, *"No my actual name is Malborh."* As he stops using his magic entirely and transforms into his original form in a dark elf.

This news shocked everyone because they have heard of Malborh in history. He was the dark elf that freed the prince of Chaos and killed many people before he disappeared after a huge battle with the great Elurian. All of the Amazonians picked up their weapons and pointed them at Malborh. A move he was expecting them to do and he did nothing in retaliation. *"This explained why one of the Psi warriors were killed quickly"* Alessia says, *"They recognized you and you did not want the secret getting out that you were still alive."* Malborh nods at her saying yes. Sebak didn't know what to say to Malborh. Because on top of him being his stepfather he was the evil that started everything.

Malborh also says, *"because of me Elurian and a dragon named Phyrra created the Dragiir to combat the evil*

*that was rising. So technically you a grandchild of an Elf &
a dragon Sebak. Not many of your race realize where you
come from because Elurian never told any of your ancestors.
I learned it while I was trying to stop my best friend from
getting ahead. Elurian and I have talked many times and I
always thought I was in the right in what I was doing. I just
didn't realize what I was doing until it was too late."*

Queen Tessa knew something was off about him and
decides to put him in a dungeon. Not giving the others time
to think and process what they just seen and heard from
Malborh's mouth. Scar and Nyssa couldn't forgive him
because he killed many of their people in the past. Many of
their ancestors paid the ultimate price at that elf's hands. The
two of them wanted Malborh dead. Alessia and Neville
became nomads because of Malborh. But they were not
upset about, in the long run it became a blessing in disguise.
So, they voted to keep Malborh with them. For Sebak
though, *"Malborh has not done anything outright to me or
my family. In fact, Malborh has raised me and taught me
everything he knows. There must be some good in him
because I could have turned evil at any time and Malborh
has prevented it on many levels. Second chances are very
hard to come by and maybe he has changed."* Sebak tells the
others.

They decide to save him from the dungeons of
Themyscira. Once they approach the queen, she tells them
that they were going to execute Malborh. It wasn't surprising
that they were going to do that because Scar and Nyssa
wanted him dead as well. They had to talk the queen down
from killing Malborh. They make a deal that once their
journey was over, he will return to be executed by the queen.

It took a lot before she let Malborh go on the rest of the adventure. When Malborh was released, he was surprised by what was happening. She tells him, "You have one special boy there. Make sure he does not die or we will execute you." He promises that he would protect Sebak with his life. This was enough for the Queen to kick them all off of her island. But they could not move Neville until tomorrow which they allowed them to stay the night. But Malborh had to stay the night in the dungeons because the Queen didn't trust him. he was okay with this because it was a small price to pay. This made them all feel better in a way that they now knew the truth. There was no longer any secret between them any longer as far as they knew.

Alessia decides to distance herself from the group and learn a few tricks from the amazons. The queen herself offered to train her because every woman should be able to defend themselves. Within a few seconds they learned that Alessia was amazing with a bow at any angel. They compared her to the god Apollo because of her bow skills. But they felt that she needed to tone up her body more to be a more effective warrior so she could adapt to anything that happened to her. She did not know what to think about the amazon training. In the end she wanted to stay because of the sisterhood on this island and the training was phenomenal. But her brother and everyone else was leaving tomorrow morning. She felt as though she must go with them.

The queen did want them out of her home but she did not see them as enemies. The only person that they did not trust was Mal. But she did not want to let them leave without them knowing their true potential. They do not trust men but they knew they could trust Neville, Scar, & Sebak. They ask the men to stay so that Alessia could get her training of the gods before she leaves. Nyssa and Scar both thought it would be good for them to train for a while when no one could find them. They could leave the prisoner in his cage for what he has done to the world. Mal did not have a word in edgewise because he knew he has done them all wrong in some way. He expected this treatment at some point on their journey and accepted it.

All of the older people wanted the young ones to stay within the magical barrier because of what was chasing them. Training them for the future and letting them decide their fates would not be so bad. Sebak, Neville, and Alessia all wanted to stay because of what the island could offer them. The amazons would not train Neville and Sebak but they wanted to train Alessia. But before anything could be done the amazons new there was still one secret that none of them knew of. This secret was very important because it had to do with Sebak's potential.

They order Mal to finish telling the truth to Sebak about what he was. Everyone except Nyssa and Scar were not surprised that there was another secret. Those two also knew the secret but did not want to tell Sebak until he unlocked his true potential. Mal did not know what to say to Sebak and he tells the Amazonians that the young man was not ready to hear what he actually is. Everyone was confused because they seemed to know something that Alessia, Neville, and Sebak did not know. This annoyed Tessa and she decided to show him a legendary room with legendary weaponry they have made over the years. They were not allowed to show men their armory but seeing how people are scared to tell the truth maybe the weapons could help the situation.

Once they opened the door to their armory chamber all three of the young ones heard a weapon calling to them. Alessia heard a call from a bow that the Amazonians call Artemis's Bow. She did not know what to make of it but her new Amazonian sisters said that they would help her learn. At first, they were not going to allow Neville to choose a weapon because they do not trust men. But the call from the weapon was very strong and when he could not come to it, the weapon found a way to him. It was a javelin that had no name from the Amazonians. It felt like he deserved the weapon.

As for Sebak a number of weapons were calling to him and he did not understand why that was. The queen herself told him that it was because your kind forged these weapons and entrusted them to us to protect. A ranger can use any weapon that he is given and you have been trained as such. The only thing that called to him the hardest was a gauntlet shield that have never seen the light of battle. The shield could split into two and be used as separate gauntlet weapons. He decides to keep the shield on his back if he needs it and holds his sword on his back as well. The queen of the Amazons decide that he needs more training to control himself.

But in order to train Sebak they all needed to know what he was capable of. Once again, they put Sebak under so he can do soul searching. This time his dark self was not in his way. While everyone was watching him in the water, they put him under by slowing his heart rate. Before he could find true serenity, he discovers a message from his father Bakari. No one could imagine what Sebak was feeling when he got see his real father for a change. Sebak did not know what to do but to hug his father because he did not get a chance to meet him until now. Even though this was all in his mind Sebak did not want to leave this moment ever. This is where Bakari informs him that they do not get to be happy. *"Heroes are doomed to die alone"* he says with much conviction.

This helps Sebak understand what happened to his father a little and it was not the full story. Bakari tells him, *"I have done many terrible things but throughout my life I have done only one great thing and that was creating you. Son, you saved me before I realized I needed saving. I was headed down a path that was wrong for the world. I learned what I was and I let it go to my head son. We are the Dragiir son. A race created by a sorcerer elf and a celestial dragon to change the fate of the world. We have power that most do not understand son. Because of it I let it go to my head and I became someone you would not be proud of. Then the titan of chaos was released because of my stupidity. To protect you and to save most of the world I had to sacrifice myself to ensure your survival."*

"I am so very sorry son. You have to bear the cross that I could not finish. I thought I killed the titan but all I did was weaken him. He is still among the living son. My sacrifice was for nothing but to give you a chance to grow up and I'm happy I was able to give you that. Your life would never have been normal because you are a Dragiir. You are carrying the torch son and I will be with you every step of the way. Do not make the same mistakes I did son."

The two of them embrace one another and there was a blinding light that awakened Sebak. The light signified true serenity for Sebak because he is no longer secretly angry about the past and why his parents aren't with him anymore. He is now truly at peace inside his soul. His anger can no longer torment him from the inside. Where anger once stood there is a new emotion and passion for the future. Wondering what it will hold for him and his new family. Sebak decides to vow to protect his new formed family no matter the cost. When he awakens, he understands what he needs to do now. They still needed to go to the find Alessia and Neville's horde.

Six months later, Nyssa and Scar were together one night and they convince one another that they will no longer live for other people but for each other. They have always done what was right for their people and the future. She shows Scar that she is pregnant with their first child. Scar felt like the happiest man on earth and felt that his honor has been rewarded. The two of them kiss one another to show joy and happiness. But he could not stay with her because his quest is not yet over. He must protect Sebak where ever the young man goes. That was the deal from his father's dying wish and he will honor it.

Meanwhile, Sebak and Neville finally finish their training after six months. Neville messing with Sebak every chance he gets and betting a few silver coins for however many times he could land a blow on Sebak. In the end of these months Sebak ended up with a hundred silver and Neville was rewarded with three hundred gold. "It's alright mate just because you're the chosen one doesn't mean you are the best at everything." Neville says to Sebak as they laugh. Sebak sees Alessia sitting in the tree alone and Neville knew what that meant and he decided to leave the area to give Alessia and Sebak some space. Sebak was curious as to why she was sitting alone in a tree.

As soon as Sebak asked her what was wrong she turned around in tears. She informs him, *"Neville is not her brother but her half-brother. While training all this time neither of us knew about our mother or father. They learned who I was because of this mark on my back. They learned that my mother was once an Amazonian before she became a nomad steppe warrioress. To many of the people here they believe that I am the daughter of a god named Hephaestus a Greek god of metalworking, artisans, fire, and volcanoes. Can you believe that Sebak?"* with this news he did not know what to say. But he attempts to comfort her in any way possible. He holds her and she lays her head on his chest. She could hear his heartbeat matched hers.

Sebak says, *"Just because they say that Neville is not your brother it does not make him any less so. He has been there for you sense you both were born. And he is still here with you now on this journey. He is your brother no matter what. Blood does not bond you as family. sometimes family can come from anywhere. It's about who you trust and who has your back when you are at your darkest hour. Neville loves you as a sister and would do anything to see you happy, I am sure. Do not worry about it Alessia just be happy to know the true information about where you come from. I still do not know who my mother is. The woman that took care of me all my life still feels like my true mother. Because she was there when no one else was. But my blood mother is out there somewhere ruling a kingdom and did not have time for me. One day I will learn the full truth."*

In the heat of the moment Alessia looks up at Sebak and the two share their first kiss. Sebak was completely caught off-guard by this movement. But it was a welcome one because he did not know how she truly felt about him until now. He did not stop her the two continued to kiss each other for a while until an Amazonian came looking for Alessia. Her training was not complete. The Amazonian interrupted their tender moment without hesitation.

Once Alessia walked away to begin her training for the day. The Amazonian stops Sebak and tells him, "You are the reason that she cannot reach her full potential. You must leave this island at once if you at all care about her." Then she walks away not giving Sebak a change to argue the situation. Annoyed by what the Amazonian had said to him and it not being the first one to say this to him over the course of the six months. He decides to go find Scar and the rest of them. He informs them that they have overstayed their welcome here and must leave. They ask about Alessia and her training and he dismisses it and says that we are in her way. He storms down to the dungeons and goes to get Mal. The warriors did not understand what was going on. But he informs them that all of them were leaving except Alessia.

The gear up and were ready to leave Sebak looks at Alessia but he did not want to disturb her while she was training. Neville didn't feel right about just up and leaving Alessia like this. But Sebak was ready to go because of the treatment that the Amazonians were beginning to give him. Neville did not want to leave Alessia behind but the Amazonians assure them that she is safer there than she would ever be with them. Then they secretly force the entire group off of the island. Scar and Mal knew it would happen eventually because the Amazonians do not trust men. Especially those with royal blood in their veins. Sebak leaves without looking back. They were set on their path once again.

Once they were a few miles out everything was quiet and something did not seem right. Everyone was on horseback and riding through a forest. Everyone was on edge because something did not seem right. Then a figure drops from the trees landing on one knee. He slams his left hand into the ground making a magical shock wave knocking everyone and almost everything over. The horses fall to the ground and some land on their riders. Mal recognizes the assailant and does not know what to do.

CHAPTER 8: THE AMBUSH & THE HORDE

The Assailant draws his sword upon Mal and he recognizes that it was an elven scimitar weapon. A weapon that is not often seen any more in this new world. Scar was attending to Nyssa and could not help Mal. Neville was knocked unconscious because he fell off of the horse and hit a tree. Sebak was trying to get from under his dead horse. Mal had no choice but to fight the assailant one on one. Scar wanted to help Mal but he did not want to leave his wife and child. Mal begins to battle the assailant and he was put on defensive immediately by the assailant. Using magic to create a sword to fight him one on one. But while clashing Mal realized who he was dealing with and his style of fighting from the past.

When he created an opening knowing that the assailant was after him, Mal decides to stop the fight and run away from the area making the assailant follow him through the forest. Sebak just gets up at that moment and chases after them. Mal far out in front and the assailant on his tail. Sebak was chasing both of them and not far behind. The three of them run through the forest like they knew the area. Mal runs into a heard of horses and it makes them all run the same direction. Mal jumps on the back of one of the horses and uses magic to calm it down. He uses the horse to outrun his attacker. Sebak does the same thing and jumps on a horse also. When Sebak ride past the assailant he jumps on the back of the horse that Sebak was on. The three of them end up separating from the heard of horses.

Fighting with the assailant Sebak discovers that the assailant is a sea elf. A race once thought long destroyed and forgot centuries ago. From his appearance he seemed to be very old for an elf. But he seemed very skilled for the age that he looked by Sebak's observation. The elf uses magic to frighten the horse and make it fall over, using the momentum of the falling horse he jumps towards Mal that was ahead of them.

Sebak did not fall easily and within one single fluid motion jumps to his feet and begins to run after the elf and Mal. The elf on the other hand uses the momentum to slash at the horse causing it and Mal to fall. The Elf stands over Mal and says, *"I have finally caught up to you Malborh. You will pay for all of your crimes."* But before he could go for the killing blow Sebak leaps and tackles the elf sending the both rolling a little way away. Sebak positions himself between the elf and Mal showing that he would protect Mal. But before the two could begin fighting they seemed to have landed inside of an ambush from a steppe horde. The horde surrounded them and told them to lay their weapons down.

The elf lays down his weapons and introduces himself to them all. He informs them that he Elurian the great elf that once tried to save this world. The Steppe knew who he was and they apologized for the hostility immediately. But they could not allow anyone just to breach their camp perimeter without fighting back. They figure out that Sebak was protecting Mal and they kept their weapons on them. They wanted Sebak to surrender the villain for all of his wrong doings. Before the situation escalated Sebak was joined by Neville. Meanwhile, Mal was smirking and laughing to himself. He only does so to not draw attention to himself. In his mind, *"These fools have actually warmed up to me. These children know nothing."*

They all recognize Neville's face and puts their weapons down. Neville signals Sebak to do the same. He informs Sebak that these are my people. Once Neville showed his face the queen arrived to the situation as well along with the new Khan of their clan. Morven was not happy that none of them were keeping their eyes on Mal because he is the trickster here. Neville has a heartfelt reunion with his mother and step-father. Before Morven could make a move on Mal everyone was invited into the camp. The Khan made that an order so everyone had to obey it even the prisoners.

Meanwhile, back at the kingdom of Vanalaos the Emperor Morkere and his son Sansom is meeting with his father the Emperor of Chaos, Aethos. He was annoyed with the progress that they have had lately and losing the daughter of a Greek god. But Aethos learns that there has been an awakening. *"A Dragiir is alive and well. We must turn him to our favor like we did the first one. We must crush and corrupt his heart. And drive him mad. Only then will we kill him after he watches everything he loves dies. But considering I cannot seem to count on you all to do anything correctly. I will send my trusted advisor Jarin Mousse."* The wizard teleports to them as they were speaking to the Emperor of Chaos.

He leaves the wizard in charge of his own son and grandson. but the wizard was not alone either. He brings his own order with him called the Order of Destruction. The order of destruction was four individual knights that were knighted by the Titan himself and granted specific magical abilities to enhance their skills. The wardens; Sir Dawkins, Sir Perez, Sir Roule, & Sir Hamon four of the last warriors you would ever see in battle. Jarin smiles because he knows he has free reign to do what he pleases with the problem at hand. He begins to lay down the plan for the titan's child and grandson. while he began to use magic to create a platoon of orc like creatures to fight the coming battle.

The wizard also recruited the Psi warriors help as well to complete this impossible task that they have set in front of them. Their mission was to keep these so-called heroes separated and unable to communicate with one another. While the order moved in to destroy them with a platoon of orc like creatures at their backs. The wizard was very pleased with his plan but he did not take his opponents likely and decided to create contingency plans as best as possible. They were going to capture the demigod woman and deliver her to their lord and master Aethos no matter the cost…

Back in the forest, Elurian was not out to make friends he made it known that his only mission was rid the world of Mal. He tells Sebak, *"I as ask you as warrior to warrior. How long can you keep your so-called step-father safe from me?"* giving Sebak a death stare. Sebak answers his threat with a death stare of his own. But the two would not stay near each other for long. They learn that the Steppe people also picked up Scar and his wife Nyssa. Sebak was happy to see that they both were alright and nothing happened to Nyssa and Scar's child. He walks up to them and puts his head on Nyssa's stomach. He tells the little one, *"You have wonderful parents. They are the strongest people I know. and your father is the wisest man I ever met. You are very blessed little one."*

Sebak's words made both Nyssa and Scar happy and they hug him. Neville was not too happy to be back with his people so quickly. But in the end, you have to do what you have to do. He begins to tell Sebak one of the reasons why he left his people was because he was not ready to be a Khan. But Sebak being himself he says, *"Responsibility is rarely thrust upon us when we are ready. It usually happens when we do not think we are ready for it. Only to show us that we are my friend. Don't be so quick to shake the responsibility, Neville. You make like it better than being a sell sword. Tell me how can you be a sell sword and not actually use a sword?"* Mocking him. Neville never thought of it that way but once he began to mock him the two started horseplaying for a while.

It wasn't long before the sky turned dark due to the use of dark magic. They Steppe people realized that they were about to have an unwelcome guest and decided to ready their warriors. They even released Mal and Elurian from their bonds so they could help fight. The wizard Jarin Mousse arrives through a dark portal and it remained open behind him. he introduces himself telling everyone his name and who he worked for.

Jarin also tells them that he is not the time bore everyone with speeches. To save everyone a monologue he just decides to tell them to *"Die"* and a platoon of orc like creatures come pouring out of the portal. The creatures struck fear into the hearts of many because of how ugly they were. None of them knew what to do exactly because they all wanted to run. But the moment was struck upon Neville and his step-father. Before the Khan could give hope to his men Neville stepped in for him. He tells them, *"I know you all are scared I am too. We did not mean to bring this hell down upon you all it just happened this way. But the horde of hell is upon us. What did our forefathers do when they were upon them? They did not turn tail and run they stood the devil himself in the face and said... Not today demon. Are we or are we not their descendants?"* the steppe shout in agreement that they are.

Neville continues, *"Then why don't we give them a fight they will never forget."* Giving a command in their native language all of the soldiers form a shield wall and the archers were ready to fire. The Khan was proud of his step son and how much he has grown and queen was proud as well. Neville's order tells them to pick off some of them one by one. Keep them at bay. Sebak stood next to Neville to help him feel empowered by what was about to happen. The Khan gives the order open fire entirely to keep the enemy back.

The wizard did not expect this much fight coming from simple field humans. Through the portal he created more of them and made seem like there was an endless amount of them. Mal sees what would become a problem was the Portal and he knew what would come after the wizard. He decides to fly up to the wizard and engage him one on one. Upon doing so the two began to fight with their magic. The wizard protecting the portal by keeping Mal away from it. Mousse called Mal, *"TRAITOR!!!!"* as the two threw lighting and every other element they could think of at each other.

Nyssa was in no condition to fight having a child leaving Scar no choice but to protect his wife and child. He had an obligation to Sebak but he also had one to his wife and child. Nyssa was already leading the children of the steppe from the battlefield and she was leaving with them. Scar decides to go with them to make sure they make it away from the battlefield. While there leaving the run into two of the wardens from the Order of destruction. Sir Hamon and Sir Perez. The two of them love feeding off of the weak and their fear. Scar tells his wife and the children to run as he stands between them and the enemy. They laugh and say, *"No Naga can defeat us young one. Many have tried and many have failed. You will fall all the same."*

Scar takes off his tunic and puts his weapon on his side. He uses the dirt at his feet to wash his hands and pray. Scar prays, *"Gods forgive me for what I am about to do. I promised I would never use my full potential again unless needed. But it is for my wife and child. For them I would do anything to see a future with them. I will never be ashamed to want peace with my family."* as the two wardens ready themselves to fight this old warrior. Scar holds his sheath with his left hand and the handle of his Scimitar with his right hand. In the blink of an eye Scar covers eighty feet in the matter of one second. Luckily Warden Perez was able to block the attack off instinct alone. The both of them were shocked at the speed of the old warrior.

But Sir Perez was excited to finally have a real opponent that could test his skills. Sir Hamon was attempting to stay on Scar but he and Perez were both moving extremely quickly. Unbelievably Scar was holding them both at bay with only one hand on his scimitar. He stood in the center of both of them swinging his arm in all directions blocking both of their attacks with one hand. Sir Hamon being on his left and Sir Perez on his right. All Scar could think about at the time was him waiting for his family and the innocent to be far enough away before began to fight for real.

Back in Themyscira Alessia could feel Neville and Sebak being in danger. She was severely annoyed that the Amazonians pushed them away from her. They would keep saying that her training was not complete. But she did not care about that right now because her family was in danger while she is in a protective magical shield. Alessia aggressively shows how angry at them she was becoming. And the stronger her emotions the more the fire around her grew. Her power was growing to the point that the ground began to shake. Queen Tessa tells her, *"Enough young one."* But Alessia retaliates, *"No! I will not just sit here and let my brother and the man I love die because you want to keep me here to hide me from the titan. They should have a chance too."*

Alessia begins to walk away from the training field but is stopped by the queen. Queen Tessa tells Alessia, *"STOP! Or you will never be queen of Themyscira."* Alessia stops in her tracks confused. Tessa looks Alessia in her face and says, *"You are more like me than I ever thought you would be."* Alessia had to put two and two together after she said this and did not know how to react. All she could say was, *"No... no... no... you are supposed to be dead."* Alessia runs away from the training field and begins to pack so she could help her new family. Queen Tessa allows her to leave without anyone stopping her because that news was not something you take likely.

Tessa walks into her room and tries to talk to Alessia. But she did not care about anything Tessa had to say because forever she thought that she was dead. For half of her life, she thought that she was dead because she never came back to them. She didn't have time to process the information because she wanted to help Neville and Sebak. Tessa says, *"It's okay if you want to help you friends. It's the hero in your daughter. If this is what you truly want, we will go to war. But if you do not want it, we will stay here."*

Back on the battlefield, Neville and the warriors hold the line shooting the orc like creatures down. In the end they knew they could not hold them back forever. They would have to engage them at some point why not now. Everyone waited for the Khan to give the order. But he gives the opportunity to Neville because one day he will have to know how to be a khan on the battlefield. Nervous he looks at Sebak and then looks at Mal fighting the wizard flying around in the sky. He looks back to see if the young children and all the innocent defenseless people are gone. Then he looks at all the men and women ready to fight and die for their people. It began to empower him more seeing all those brave faces about to face death itself with no hesitation.

He steps out from the shield wall and yells, *"For the HORDE!"* everyone yells those words with him in agreement. They all begin to charge as Neville is out in front of everyone. Both armies charge at one another without no hesitation. Neville wanting to prove he is worthy by being all the way out in front. As they are running both Sebak and Elurian catches up to Neville before he hits the enemy. The three of them running side by side engage the enemy at the same time. Neville throwing his javelin at the first creature within twenty feet of him. when the javelin returned to him, he stabs his second kill in the face. Elurian slashes all that comes to him getting a higher kill count quicker because of his elven speed. Sebak using his shield & Spear technique to fight off every creature that lunge at him.

The rest of the army engage the enemy right after the heroes do and there is a huge clash of metal and bones breaking. Neville and Sebak were in cohesion as they were battling these creatures. Whenever one went high the other would go low without even speaking to one another. They cover each other's blind spots with ease and fluid motions. It was like the two of them were one. No one was giving up the fight no matter the odds that they were facing. They were fighting for their future.

CHAPTER 9: BATTLE OF THE TRIBES

In the sky, Mal and Mousse battle with the extent of their magical knowledge. All Mal knew was that he must keep this wizard away from the others at all costs. He was too powerful for them at their current level. All Mal could say was, "I will protect them with my life no matter what happens." He begins to laugh at what he had just said. He knew being a hero was easy to fake. It was priceless to him and he did not care about them at all. Mousse would grow confused and did not understand what was happening. Mal would tell him, "This is all a trick. I want to be close to the boy to watch him grow and feed off of his power. He has so much power… so does the young amazon woman. Let me show you."

Mousse would throw spells at Mal and he would counter them with something else. It seemed that both understood their limits of magic and what they could throw at one another. At one point Mousse throws a huge fireball at Mal and he counterattacks with turning the fireball into glass and throwing it back at Mousse. Mousse was not expecting this change and was cut in multiple places by the glass. Mal having something to counter Mousse for every attack annoyed him by all means. But he must stall long enough for the demigod girl to arrive so they can ambush her.

But little does he know that two of the wardens are having trouble in the forest with a Naga warrior named Scar. The plan was unfolding without Mousse even knowing. But he was doing not take failure as an option. He could see on the ground that the battle was in their favor no matter how many of those creatures the humans kill they will keep coming. from where he was looking it looked as though the humans were beginning to tire out. He began to smirk because this battle was almost over for them.

But little did they know what was about to happen on the battlefield. Queen Tessa and Alessia arrive with the Calvary from Themyscira. They did not expect the entire Amazonian army to arrive to assist the horde. This surprised Jarin Mousse but he had already planned for them just in case. But Mal would not allow him time to think because he knew keeping him off the battlefield would give the humans and his family a chance. Mal was starting to irritate the wizard Mousse.

On the battlefield, the Amazonian army arrives just in time to help the steppe horde. Neville and Sebak were happy to see Alessia once again. They did not know what would have happened if she never showed up. The three of them share a small moment on the battlefield. Alessia punches her brother in the arm a little just to tell him, "Never leave without saying goodbye again brother." As the two hugs on the field of battle. Neville reassured her that it would never happen again. Neville goes back to fighting after greeting his sister. Then when she gets to Sebak she slaps him for leaving and being angry. Because she heard about how he reacted to their treatment. But she also kisses him because she missed his presence.

The two team up on the battlefield once their reunion was done properly. The two of them were more fluid than Sebak and Neville were. The two did not have to speak to one another to know what the other was about to do. It was almost like a dance while they were on the battlefield. They killed many of the creatures before sharing a passionate kiss on the battlefield. Neville standing nearby tells them, "Oh come on it is not the time for that!" as he and others are knee deep in enemies. Alessia stops using her blades and begins to use her Artemis bow. She was capable of shooting multiple arrows at a time dropping many enemies from behind Sebak. He became her shield and keep the enemy from getting too close to her.

Meanwhile, Scar was fighting the two wardens once he realized that the innocent children and his wife were out of harm's way, he began to let loose a little on the enemy. He separated them almost easily and used their number advantage against them. Sir Perez could see what he was beginning to do and did not care he was having fun with this old warrior. At one point Sir Hamon and Sir Perez had Scar sandwiched between them. Perez was going to block Scar's attack while Hamon attacked from behind. But Scar manages to dodge Perez's attack and spins his blade backwards and thrusts his blade into Hamon's stomach by surprise.

Sir Perez was not fazed by Hamon being stabbed in the stomach at all. Scar removes the blade from Hamon's stomach and moves to regroup. Perez was annoyed that Hamon even got hit by this mortal. He decides that Hamon is a disgrace to their race and he kills him by snapping Hamon's neck and removes his head. In anger not realizing he just showed Scar how to kill them. Something no other being or person has been able to do once Aethos knighted them. But Perez tells Scar, "Finally... I do not have to hold back anymore." Scar agrees and says, "Oh you have no idea." As the two readied themselves in their stances. Scar realized that Perez changed his style once Hamon was no longer in the fight. But he was not concerned about it at all. The two began to move so quickly that if you were to blink before they moved you would not know what happened.

Back on the battlefield, the battle was beginning to change once again to the enemies' favor. The final two wardens arrived on the battlefield and they were not alone. They brought the psi warriors with them as well. Seeing these new fresh warriors joining the battle the Khan of the horde tells everyone to fall back now. The Amazonians attempt to help them escape and retreat at the same time themselves. Sir Roule ended up engaging the Khan because he was holding his wife hostage. But the Khan had no chance against a titan's chosen.

Neville sees this and wanted to help his mother and step-father. Sebak clears the way and puts his shield together on one arm and puts it over his head. He knew what Sebak was signaling and runs towards Sebak and steps on the shield so he could launch him towards his family. Neville does a corkscrew spin in the air and lands on his feet in a fluid motion and runs to his mother and father. He intercepts Roule before he could kill his step-father. The relief of seeing Neville was enough for the Khan to collapse on the ground from his injuries. He was proud of what his step-son had become.

Sir Boulevard and Sir Fulchard finds Alessia and Sebak on the field and confront them. They were not alone either deciding to use their new recruits of psi warriors to outnumber the two of them. Alessia and Sebak smile but they were not ready for what was to come. Enough psi warriors on the same wavelength could be unstoppable. Both Alessia and Sebak could sense what they were about to do and why. but Sebak knocks them all down to give Alessia a chance to open fire on them all. The leaders blocked the attacks but the recruits were not so fortunate. Alessia jumped in the air and shot multiple arrows in multiple directions as she spins in the air before she hit the ground again.

Sir Boulevard was still impressed with Alessia and says, "That is why I must have you. The titan wants you because of your ties to the Greek god. But I want you for something more meaningful." He says with a smirk. Sebak wanted to kill him for her but she stops him. she says, "Let me do this. I need to end this myself. Just watch my back love." As she readies her bow to fight him. Boulevard attempts to use his telekinesis on the bow and its arrows, he could not affect her weapons for some reason. It took the smirk off of his face very quickly. Alessia informs Boulevard, "I expected you or anyone else to attempt to do something like that. I put runes on my weapon to ward against unfair advantages from my enemies."

Aggressively Boulevard lunges at Alessia making her go on the offensive. She shot arrow after arrow at him until he was upon her. She then drew her short sword and dagger to block him. putting away her bow was where she lost the advantage but the runes on the bow allowed her a little advantage even when it is not drawn. They clash for a while blade to blade and for a second, they seemed even but Alessia's face told a different story. She could tell that she was entirely in his head. But then he disarms her with his telekinesis and uses telekinetic lightning on her that was entirely unexpected.

Sebak watched as the woman he loved and the man she hated battled like never before. Sir Fulchard decided to attempt a sneak attack on him while he was not paying attention. But Sebak quickly blocked with his shields that now were in the form of a kite shield when they are together. With ease Sebak could switch arms that the shield was on to throw off his opponents. Fulchard was using a longsword to fight Sebak and he seemed to be completely outclassed by Sebak in skill. The shield transformed in mid motion into a circular shield so Sebak could throw it at Fulchard. All of Sebak's movements and fighting style was throwing the old man off. He had never faced someone so unorthodox. Sebak smirks a little because he could feel that he has come a long way.

The fight comes down to one crucial moment for Sebak and Fulchard. The warden lunges at him and thrust his sword towards Sebak's face. But he manages to move entirely out of the way by ducking the attack. Before Fulchard could stop the attack Sebak puts the shield on his right arm and uppercuts the sword while it was being thrusted at him. the sword shatters and it surprises Fulchard and the shock of the uppercut and the blade breaking knocks him off of his feet. He did not know what else to do but surrender to Sebak after his blade was destroyed.

Once Sebak's guard was down Fulchard attempts to stab him in the leg but Sebak was ready for underhanded strikes and blocks it. He counters with the shield as it transforms back into a kite shield and stabs Fulchard in the face killing him. Sebak goes back to supporting the army and fighting the orc like creatures. Neville on the other hand was fighting Sir Roule and doing well for a man that does not have any magical powers. While Neville was fighting Roule his mother was holding her husband on the battlefield. She could not move him because he would die from his injuries. He decides to name as his successor and let it be known that he is the new khan among their people.

Without Neville knowing his step-father dies slowly in the arms of his loving wife. Neville felt his mother cry and turned around to see his step-father dead. Neville in anger gets aggressive with his fighting towards Roule. The two of them traded blows hand for hand. But Roule was in control the entire time of the fight. He tells Neville, "You have a lot to learn young one." As he fights Neville, he realizes what was happening around him. The battle was beginning to shift once again from their side back to Neville's army from Roule's perspective. The surrounding fight began to worry Roule a little.

Meanwhile, Scar and Perez are battling with everything they have. Their slashes were so quick that no one could follow their movements. Both of them were getting a few slashes on their shoulders arms and legs without realizing it. Both of them separated for a second to catch their breath. Once they did catch their breath both quickly lunged at the other for one killing blow. They both stop on opposite ends of where they were signifying that they have both slashed at one another. Scar stood up first and Perez dropped to his knees. Perez tells Scar, "Not bad for an old man. You have my respect." As he falls over and dies from a severe slash that separated his chest from his stomach.

Scar walks away from the fight to see what was happening on the battlefield. He could see that everyone needed him so he rushed as quickly as he could back to the battlefield. His scares were not severe like Perez's were.

Leaving him capable of still fighting afterwards scar moved as fast as he could to help Sebak and the others. But while he was running Scar opened a wound that he did not feel touch him that caused him to limp towards the battlefield. Looking at the injury he could tell it was possible to heal. But his quickness has been taken from him for the rest of this battle. He did not care he bandaged it up and still headed towards the battlefield. He knew that his second family needed him so he moved as quickly as he could.

Mal and Mousse's fight was not as even as Mousse would think. He was being outsmarted and outplayed by Mal. Because of all the magic Mal was using he was beginning to cough because he was over exerting himself. This gave Mousse a chance to catch him off-guard and hit him with a sharded spears of ice. The ice skewers Mal and it makes him drop to the ground. Elurian seeing this does not believe that this was the end of Mal. He was the only one open to help Mal at this moment in time. Elurian decided not to help Mal but to help the children in their trouble. Mal tries not to scream in pain but the ice was being twisted by Mousse so he could suffer. Mousse says, "This is what happens to those that betrays the Emperor of Chaos Aethos. You will suffer slowly and die old man. You have been a thorn in my master's side for long enough. I am glad that I am the one to bring about the end of your life."

Meanwhile, Roule manages to beat Neville down because he was unbalanced after seeing one of his loved ones die. Roule manages to pick up Neville by his neck and hold him to watch him kill his mother. Neville did whatever he could to attempt to stop Roule from killing her. Neville tried to cry out for his mother to move but Roule was choking him.

It was at that moment that Neville's javelin lights up as Neville rases his hand towards his mother because he was beginning to lose hope. The javelin moves on its own and protects Neville's mother and absorbs the blast of the magical attack. This surprised Roule as Neville did not know what he just did as he was beginning to lose consciousness. The javelin then attempts to attack Roule but he dodges the attack and release Neville. Once he regroups with the javelin it glows a golden like color and separates into multiple javelins. He uses his had to control where the weapons went. He does a circular motion and then it follows his motion and then launches at Roule. With surprise Roule now could see Neville as an actual threat.

Alessia and boulevard on the other hand, Alessia was drained because of all the lightning she had absorbed. Boulevard tells her, "You put up a better fight than you ever have in the past and I commend you for trying. But now it's time for you to come home and stop pretending. Or would you rather die here?" Alessia did not answer him as he was ready to execute her for defying him. But at that same time Alessia could hear her father talking to her. He tells her, "Now is your time. You can have the blood of a god and still be a no one. You are more than just a demigod. You are a princess of the amazons. All your life you have wanted to know who you are. Now that you know who you are. Who are you?" Alessia yells out loud answering her father, "I am ALESSIA!" as volcanic lava erupts from underneath the ground with the motion of her right hand.

The lava makes Boulevard back off of her very quickly and doing so he began to fear Alessia. The lava surrounded her like a giant snake waiting for her command. Before he could speak, she signals for the lava to attack him. The lava wraps around him like a snake and then floats above him. The sides squeezing him to death while he uses his psionics to protect him from the heat. Alessia's power was way stronger than he expected it to be.

The lava snake picks up Boulevard and his psionics could no longer protect him. He began to burn everywhere and it made Alessia happy to hear him scream. Once she heard him screaming, she motions for the snake to end him. The lava snake goes to bite Boulevard and with the motion of Alessia's hand the snake puts its entire face into Boulevard and it slams him to the ground covered in lava. Once the lava seeps back into the ground there was nothing left of Boulevard. Next thing Alessia hears is Mal screaming in pain and it makes her look up to find Mal covered in ice and at the mercy of this wizard. Without hesitation Alessia goes to help Mal because he would have helped her.

Elurian decides to keep an eye on the battlefield for any surprises from Malborh because he knows that he can be conniving when it comes to a battlefield. He also could feel a demonic presence emulating from the wizard. He could not place it exactly for a moment until he fully recognized the power. It was from the titan of chaos Aethos. The idea of the titan being involved shocked Elurian. Meaning that they were truly facing a powerful enemy this time. Finally, the face of evil was going to attempt to show their face. He decides that he must watch over these young ones. Their lives may mean more than he thought originally when he first saw them. This new world has created its own heroes in the time of darkness.

"Such things are the way of the world and the balance of nature. Whenever evil rises the light will rise with it. Doing so will only balance the world once and for all. Someone will always fight with the power of love. While others will fight with the power of hatred. We must be ready for what is to come. I will not repeat what happened all those years ago." Elurian begins to leave the battlefield to prepare for the worst of it all. Knowing that the heroes will rise from this battle and they will rise the better for it all. "Something big is at play here" Elurian thought to himself as he teleported back to his home.

CHAPTER 10: POTENTIAL

Mousse tells Mal, "I always looked up to you as a young one. I always thought you were a formidable warrior. But you are dying. So, is this what happens when you have a change of heart? You become weak and fragile?" he laughs mockingly at Mal. Mal retaliates, "I have been dying ever sense Bakari and I tried to stop the Titan from escaping his bonds. I have been living one day at a time. I promised that Dragiir that I would protect his son and mold him into a warrior that could stop the titan and his army. I have achieved that. I have no reason left to live. If I go to purgatory for all that I have done so, be it. But I have done one good thing in my life." as he attempts to stand once again with the ice shards inside him.

Before Mal could make a move Mousse turns his hand to put Mal in severe pain. Mousse approaches him slowly to show Mal that he was defeated completely. Before Mousse could attempt to go for the final blow. He was tackled by Scar and Scar tells Mal, "Get out of here." As the wizard Mousse and Scar began their fight. Mal could not move because of the shards within his body. It was nothing short of miraculous that he could even stand up. He begins to see flashes of his peace of mind. He was beginning to see the light while he was standing there. Because of it he falls to the ground once again and thinks of his friends that he once had. Sebak runs to Mal once he finally got the chance to do so.

Alessia tells the army to stand down as she closes the portal stopping the unending orc like creatures from pouring out. The army kills the remaining creatures that were still running around. Roule seeing that he was now majorly out matched he decides to tell Neville, "Another day boy. You may win the battle but you will not win the war." As he fades into shadow and leaves. Neville collapses to the ground because he asserted all energy he had. "Ahh. I hurt all over!" Neville says to his mother when he falls down.

Mousse fights Scar for only a few seconds before the wizard gets the better of him. he uses the same ice magic to disable Scar like he did Mal. Because Scar was already injured it made it a lot easier for him to incapacitate Scar. The ice inters all of his injuries in the matter of seconds making Scar fall to his knees before Mousse. He creates a weapon out of ice to execute Scar once and for all. Mousse says, "You have been an annoyance sense you were the bodyguard of Bakari. Good thing we never caught up with you until now. Our you would have never been a threat at all. Life has been kind to you Scar. Too bad I am about to end it." As he swings for Scar's head Alessia kicks Mousse in the face with a flying kick.

Scar was weakened fighting Perez and then fighting an omega level threat afterwards was not smart even for Scar. Sebak could not get his head in the game because he was seeing all of his friends and the people, he loves fall. He was frozen with fear of seeing Mal, Neville, and Scar so injured. Mal and Scar both try to convince Sebak, "It is alright to be afraid. Many things happen we knew what we're doing when we began this quest. Death is not the end Sebak. Death is nothing to fear it is a part of life. the world needs you right now son. You have been trained for this. Do not make the same mistakes as so many have done. Many have had the opportunity to grab ahold of their life and never did so. Are you going to be like them?" Sebak says, "No." Scar finishes Mal's speech for him, "Then if that is the case who are you?" Sebak says his name but he whispers it.

Mal says to Sebak weakly, "You are more than just what your parents were. You have all of their blood and hold their mistakes because you have their name. but in the end, it is what you do with your life that matters my boy. You are more than just a boy in the shadow of his father, you are your own man. Right now, you're allowing your fear to overtake you and allow the woman you love to fight your battle. You are not weak Sebak you are stronger than evil."

Sebak snaps out of the fear that he was feeling of losing everyone and moves to help Alessia. Alessia and Sebak stood side by side after she managed to knock him back. They decide to fight Mousse together and end this once and for all. Everyone else were tending to the wounded finally got too Mal and Scar. They removed them from the battlefield but the two did not stop watching Alessia and Sebak. Mal and Scar both were proud of what they have become. In the beginning they didn't know each other know they have become a family of their own making. Scar passes out and Mal fades away while watching Alessia and Sebak battle. Mal died at peace because he knew the world was in good hands with the three of these young warriors.

Mousse disarms Alessia and Sebak in the beginning of the fight because they were not capable of moving as quick as Mousse is without any weapons in his hand. Then Alessia and Sebak look at one another to get on the same page. Mousse tells them, "No matter how many different ways you come at me you will not be able to defeat me." without speaking Alessia goes to Mousse's right and Sebak goes to his left. The two began to punch and kick at him in unison. Mousse was left with nothing but defense for the moment because he could not cast spells with them so close to him. for every attack Alessia made Sebak answered with an equal attack keeping Mousse unable to retaliate in any way.

If Alessia kicked or punched with her left side Sebak would do so with his right. If she used her right side Sebak would use his left side. The two of them were keeping Mousse from attacking for a while until he finally found their opening by throwing Alessia one way and Sebak the other creating one. It was when they were separated was when Mousse had the chance to go on the offensive. Using powerful magic, the wizard changed dimensions on them but the fighting broke his concentration. He ended up using magic to create a platform for them to fight on in the sky so he did not have to levitate anymore.

With the magic holding the platform he did not have to hold back on them any longer. He manages to knock Sebak to the ground and he tried to pin him down so he could fight Alessia but he was very strong physically. Meaning he did not have much time and he had to knock Alessia out and complete his mission. Alessia put up more of a fight than the wizard thought she would. She was capable of earth bending and the magical platform that he made was no help for him. the only advantage he had was that she could not use lava from where they are in the air. Mousse manages to injure Alessia with his ice magic by accident while Sebak was trying to recover from being winded. He looks up and sees Alessia has stopped fighting and has a huge slice in her side. She hits the ground and was knocked unconscious from the injury.

Mousse confident that he was going to win this fight because one of them was now down. He began to boast but Sebak couldn't hear him. all he was doing was staring at the unconscious body of Alessia and seeing her injured. That was his biggest fear was losing the one he loved and he just had a taste of it seeing her knocked out. Sebak's rage overtook him finally his serenity was no more. His eyes turned completely black and his armor began to fall off of him. His skin was no longer human skin by transforming into scales. He developed scales all over his entire body. His eyes changed color to a dark red color. His voice changed into a draconic voice. He tells Mousse, "You have made a deadly mistake."

Sebak lets out a huge roar that scares everyone on the ground and Mousse himself. Because Mousse has faced many things but a fully powered Dragiir was titan level problems. But he could not let Sebak know that he feared the Dragiir and he continued to attack him. Sebak engages him and fights harder than he was before. Mousse was unable to concentrate because of his fear. He had to summon creatures to assist him and yet they did not last long because Sebak wanted to kill the wizard for hurting the people he loves.

Sebak did not care about anything anymore and wanted to rip every creature apart that the wizard created. Mousse tries to use lightning magic on Sebak because he knew fire would not work on him. But Sebak manages to get out of the way of the attack and catch his hand. The lightning showed that it was capable of disintegration as it was cutting through the platform. Mousse did everything in his power to escape this new dragon. But Sebak breaks the wizards left arm and proceeds to beat his face in with his bare hands. Draconic Sebak then picks him up with his right arm only choking Mousse to death. The platform begins to fall apart because of the damage it sustained. Sebak did not want anything more than to destroy Mousse.

Until he sees Alessia falling past him unconscious and it snaps him out of his blinding rage. The choice of saving Alessia over killing the wizard was a simple one for him. he could always kill him later on but there is only one Alessia in his life. he lets go of the wizard and sky dives after Alessia. Mousse teleports away from the battle using his one arm. Sebak did everything he could to catch her before she hit the ground. He did anything that would boost his speed of falling to get to her. But having no wings meant that he would possibly die once he touched the ground. But he wanted to give Alessia a fighting chance at least. All he could think about is, "I am here for a reason. If I cannot save the woman, I love then who am I? my life is meaningless without her in it. Alessia is my world and I will not let my world die today."

He manages to catch Alessia upon doing so he puts his back to the ground to protect her from the shock of hitting the ground. He thought, "If I am to die to day. Then let it be for someone I love. Alessia is worth dying for. Too bad I would never get the chance to tell her that I love her." As they freefall to the ground he decides to whisper in her ear, "I love you" when he says this, she begins to open her eyes. She tells him, "I love you too. Now and forever." Not realizing what was about to happen to them.

Out of nowhere as they were falling a huge creature manages to appear from under the ground and catches them.

Both Alessia and Sebak were confused about what was happening. Then it dawned on Sebak that this must be the animal that he is bonded with. It was a giant snake the size of Jörmungandr. This was a rare species and thought long dead. But apparently, they were not gone from the world. Alessia and Sebak share a passionate kiss from the two of them telling one another that they love each other for the first time. While they were kissing Sebak was able to heal her when he moved his arm over her wound. He did so without realizing it, Alessia had to tell him that she was no longer in pain. When she looks away from him and then looks back at him, he was human again without scales.

Alessia was confused because he was just a scaled dragon a second ago. But obviously Sebak did not have control over what had just happened. The three of them fly to the remaining army that they have. The day was won but at what cost many said. Because they lost many lives to fight constructs that didn't even matter. This only meant that the enemy was stronger in every way possible and they have not even faced the titan. Everyone was surprised by the gigantic griffin but it fully meant that Sebak has almost completed his journey in the world. Now he had one last task in front of him that no one could help him with. Sebak and Alessia are dropped by the griffin and the griffin leaves without a word.

Sebak did not understand what the appearance of the griffin meant but Scar did. Alessia is taken into one of the tents and her wounds are seen to. While Sebak is being treated as well but he has time to talk to Scar. The entire time Sebak thinks about Mal and how he should have been there for him. Scar puts his hand on his shoulder and tells him that the moment could not be helped. "He was ready to go and for a noble cause this time." Scar says. "This victory was not what it seems it is just the beginning and I can feel it." Sebak tells Scar.

Sebak started to drop tears because Mal was not his father but he was someone that was close enough to be one considering that he has always been there for him. Scar is like a mentor and a father figure to Sebak. "Either one of you dying would hurt me Scar. I did not need either of you to die on me. I feel like a failure." Sebak tells Scar. Scar answers, "No you are not a failure. You have only just begun your story young one. Your power is strong. You will change the world but you must be careful that your journey does not change your heart. With that being said I have for filled my mission and helped you see through your first battle and to the end of your journey. Now you know where you must go and I cannot accompany you there. You are a good man Sebak never forget that. I must see to my family from now on." Scar says.

Sebak had no hard feelings about Scar wanting to leave the fight because he has been in the fight a lot longer than many. He now has a family to think of and it would be wrong to ask him to stay away from his family any longer. Scar lets him know that even that he will not be at his side that he will always be there for him. if he needs a guiding hand any further, he tells him where they are going to stay. Then Scar shakes Sebak's hand and hugs him. Scar and Nyssa leaves the camp leaving the fight all together in the hands of Sebak. He drops a tear for his mentor leaving and living a happy life for once. Peace is the goal for every woman and man in this world. One day he will achieve true peace by destroying the titan Aethos. Sebak sets his sights on his next mission.

Sebak goes to check on Alessia only to discover that she has lost some blood to the wizard. Mousse took a sample of her blood which everyone was a little confused about why he would do that. But the important thing right now was that she was okay and would recover. Sebak kisses her on the forehead and tells her that he was going to check on Neville and he would be right back.

While everyone is feeling happy about winning this one battle Queen Tessa looks for a quiet place to hide her transgressions. The queen secretly kills off the queen of the horde to stay close to the new Khan Neville. Knowing that no one would ever suspect her involvement. Tessa hides the body of the queen in the woods and buries the body. Using this time to decide to report her mission to her queen. She shapeshifts into her true form and that was of the Naga race. She uses some sort of crystal to put on the ground to communicate with someone. The crystal creates a magical hologram that reveals the mastermind behind splitting up Alessia, Neville, and Sebak. The mastermind was working in the shadows the entire time was the Queen of the Nagas named Khesei.

She tells Tessa, "You have done well chameleon. You have earned your place among us young one. But your mission is not over yet. You have separated those so-called heroes for me. now you must bring my son Sebak to me and I do not care how you do it. As for the little girl. You must keep her away from my son." Khesei says with resentment. Chameleon responds, "I have tried to keep the two apart but their bond is strong. I have to be careful or it could change their future. Sebak has the potential to become worse than his father was. The boy is powerful and so is the young woman Alessia. This kind of thing takes time my queen. But I will complete your mission my queen." The meeting ends and Chameleon goes back to the village as Neville's mother.

Before doing so she informs the rest of the Amazonians of what the mission is from now on. It is to keep them all separated so queen Khesei can complete her goals. Their goal is to make Alessia a queen of the amazon even though their true loyalty will be to the Naga Queen Khesei. With Chameleon within both communities, they had to replace her when she leaves to mess with Neville's head. Only to keep Alessia from finding out the truth about the Amazonians.

Sebak goes to check on Neville and he discovers that they have already gone through with the ceremony for him to become. He did not know if he should bow or what to Neville now because he is a king technically. A man not named as a king because they do not believe a man can ever be called one. As a result, they came with idea of being named a Khan without angering the gods. Neville was not happy with receiving the honor in this manor but the situation could not be helped. The khan was dead and they need a new ruler and naturally the turn to the Khan's child. Neville being of age makes him the perfect choice if no one is willing to step up and claim the throne from him. After his noble speech and acts on the battlefield no one was going to challenge Neville Khan.

Neville informs Sebak, "No you should never kneel before anyone my friend. You saved us all from the wizard. You almost gave up everything that you know and love for all of us. For that I thank you. You even conquered your fear when we all needed you most." He hugs Sebak and then tells him that he was going to tell Alessia the good news. Smiling with a little worry in his eyes because he did not know if he could be a leader. Sebak tells him, "You will be okay my friend if you are capable of leading them into battle you are capable of leading them into a better life." as Neville walks away from him to see his sister. Sebak began to think about the events that has transpired around them. He started to wonder what it all meant and knew that they were here for a reason.

Neville hugs his sister even though she was injured but it was not a severe injury. They two were happy that they made it after that huge battle. He tells her that he is the new Khan of their people and it made both of them happy. But then the fact that they will have to separate sunk into their hearts. Neville lets his sister know that no matter how far apart they are he will always be her brother and will not hesitate to help her.

Then Sebak walks in to look at both of his friends one last time before they separate on their own journeys. All he could think about was that he was a lucky man to have met such fortunate people on this journey through life. Even though this all began with Mal paying them to save him. But he couldn't have expected them to become a family on this journey through to their people. Many things have changed over the course of six months and their time together have done nothing but bring them closer. Which made Sebak wonder what would happen between Alessia and him now that they will not be together for a while. It was subject he did not want to bring up to her while the three of them were together and happy.

They have lost many people in this battle and they lost the man that brought them together. Before anyone went anywhere, Neville decided to do a funeral for all those that were lost in this battle. They burned the bodies of the people that were killed in the battle. As for Mal his body disappeared entirely as if he was older than he said he was. He turned into dust and his soul flew away. It showed that he had a soul and it was no longer corrupted. He had finally ended his own torment and could be at peace. Sebak was the most heartbroken about the situation but Scar was there to comfort him before he left with his family. Neville and Alessia felt like they lost a friend and a mentor in Mal.

The next day all of them were heading their own separate ways. But they were accompanying one another until their path took them another way. They left Neville Khan with his people. Scar and his family diverged on their path into the woods and beyond. When it came down to Alessia and Sebak they did not want to let each other go. Alessia tells Sebak, "I am always yours now and forever." As the two kiss each other before they go their separate ways. Sebak did not understand it but there was a feeling that they should not part ways. They do so only for a second and Sebak returns to sweep her off her feet and make her laugh.

CHAPTER 11 THE QUEEN

Sebak did not want to let Alessia go but they had to go their separate ways. Alessia was needed in Themyscira and he needed to find his real blood mother. The two of them promises one another if anything was to happen that they would always find one another in the end. Chameleon did not like this and decided to interrupt them by telling Alessia that it was time to leave this place. It was then at that moment that Sebak could sense something was off and did not get angry with the situation. He was beginning to see things as if the Amazonians were not what they seemed. But he did not understand what was happening to him. he did not want to let go of Alessia but he had to their paths were diverging and he hoped that they would cross paths once again.

Three weeks later, Sebak arrives at Khuvia a place full of Nagas with a temple in the center of it all. They allowed him to walk right into the kingdom and they escorted him all the way to the throne room. He was very confused as to why his mother would have an entire kingdom and send him away. Anger was starting to set inside of Sebak as he walked through the Kingdom and seen all the happy faces. "Why could he not be here and grow up among them alongside his mother and father?" He asks himself this question as he walks towards the throne. This question he keeps asking himself makes him angrier and angrier as he takes a step.

He comes into the throne room full of gold ad many soldiers to protect the queen and his mother sitting on the throne. She sat on the throne with a smug grin on her face because her baby boy has finally come home. But Sebak had so many questions and so much pent-up anger as to why did she send him away if everything was fine in their home. He had to compose himself before saying anything to the woman that gave birth to him. Before he could say anything, his mother reinstates his prince hood among the Naga because of him surviving in the world.

Everyone in the throne room was surprised at what the queen said and bowed to Sebak because he would inherit the throne after she dies. Sebak did not understand what was happening here as the Queen came down from her throne and embraced him along with kissing his cheeks. She acted as if he knew who she was or their customs. But luckily Scar told him everything he needed to know of this place. He did not like his mother and she did not realize the mistake she has made. She gave him exactly what he would need to fight the titan that would come for Alessia. The Queen Khesei gave Sebak an army to use against the titan once the time came. Sebak decided he would be the prince of the kingdom but he is not her son because she forfeited the right to call him son when she gave him away.

She was sad by what he said to her but understood Sebak's anger with her because she was absent in his life. She wanted them to get reacquainted she decides to take a walk with Sebak and fill him in on the past. He was reluctant to get close to her in any way because of her leaving him. she dignified every decision she made for him to be a good reason because his father would have killed him, she informs him. but the lie did not work on Sebak because he had already met his father in the afterlife. Leaving her with no other choice but to tell the truth and tell Sebak that he was nothing but a pawn to hurt his father when he became the soul eater dragon. Because of his power she wanted to control him and it all backfired in her face to where she lost her throne to Nyssa.

Which Sebak knowing who Nyssa was he put her story together and realized that his mother staged a coup to get her throne back from Nyssa. Meaning that Nyssa is a target for his mother to kill. Also meaning that Scar would be a target for her to kill as well. He decided to tread carefully on the subject and not let her know that he knows their whereabouts. She tells him how the Naga once ruled everything in the east and it's all gone due to humanity.

Meanwhile, Mousse attempted to teleport back to his master and he was ready to report. But his spell did not work correctly it teleported him into the woods of the battlefield that he was in. He was confused as to why he could not leave the battlefield. Until he could hear an evil laugh in the distance. As the laugh gets louder everything around him shifts and he learns he has been teleported into an illusion crafted by someone. That someone was Malborh and it surprised him a lot because he thought Malborh was defeated. He says, "No… I killed you." Malborh forms in front of him and tuts at him. He responds, "Did you really think that a would-be wizard would be what would kill the great Malborh?"

He grabs the wizard by the neck and picks him up with one arm choking him to death. He explains, "The entire thing was a show you idiot. I was only trying to move the hero quicker to his goals. It seemed to have worked a little but he is not at his full potential yet. You obviously were not a real challenge for him. I sacrificed my part too early." He says beginning to make himself a little sad. "Oh well, now I get to eat your soul for my performance. A win is a win." As he begins to suck the soul out of Mousse. Mousse could do nothing to stop Malborh from taking his soul. His magic was no use in this realm that Malborh has created for himself. Mousse tried to struggle free but could do nothing as Malborh ate his soul from his body and his body goes limp.

Malborh laughs as the wizard's soul was eaten and he says to himself, "It's good to be back again. Now I can do what I like without those idiots messing anything up for me. now I must reach Hiamutt and Svalgas before it's too late." He says as he starts putting together the incantation to summon them both to him. it would take a lot of magic and it is why he absorbed the wizard's soul. It would help bring forth one of them from their prisons. Elurian was powerful once and he has been trained by the dragon of creation.

Back in Khuvia, Sebak begins to be brainwashed a little by the people around him. He knew that they were his people in every way possible. They taught him how to use all of his senses to hunt and more. Snakes are capable of a lot of things that most races did not know about. He decided to spend a lot of time with the Nagas because they were treating him like family. They taught him everything about their way of life. His eyes turned into a form of snake eyes. He felt like he actually belonged here for a change. All his life he has felt that he did not belong in the human world. In reality he was a Naga the entire time hiding among the humans. Everything began to make sense why he was superior to them in almost every way when it came to physical prowess. He still needed to learn everything like any other person but he could do so much more.

The Queen would whisper in her son's ear telling him

that humanity is the disease in this world. She shows him most of their history and shows that humanity has been the bane of their existence. They have owned these lands for generations and humanity decided to take it from them. They have been in hiding ever sense to wait for the perfect opportunity to take their ancestorial homes back. He could tell that his mother was telling the truth but not the whole truth. One thing that Scar taught him was that he should always look at the entire story not just one side of it.

The Queen realized that she had to be careful with this one because he is not easily tricked. She will have to take a different approach to the situation and gain his trust fully. But he is a very intelligent young man and he would not be easily swayed. But unluckily he has created a weakness for himself. The Queen thinks on how she will be able to exploit the situation and gain her son's love. Caution is the best move here because he has been taught how to resist her. It makes her proud that her son can't be easily tricked but it also annoys her at the same time.

Little did the queen realize what was happening within her own walls once again. Allegiance was starting to shift from her once again but in a good way for the race. This time they did so in secret because they could tell Sebak had a good heart and he cared about the people. Unlike his parents that did not care about their race whatsoever. He has a kind heart that cares about lives in general. He also wanted to blend in more with the Naga people. He learns from them how to control it but it took him months to learn how. The people loved how normal he was and how he did not want corruption for their people or to conquer anything. He just wanted peace and prosperity for everyone.

The people started to respect Sebak a lot while the loyal ones to the Queen would resent his ways. All of them believed in the old ways and would not change their ways for any new change. But some were willing to change if it meant for them to survive the change of the world. they could all sense something was coming but they did not know who would bring it or how it will come. They just know that Ragnarök was coming and they did not know when or how it was going to happen. The people that started believing that he was the one also started to look deeper into their history. They began to look into the hidden temple and learn what Sebak is to become or can become. They all felt that they needed to ready when the winds of change finally hit them.

Sebak could sense something was happening around him once again. Through the earth and sky, he could feel the seismic change around him. he could not tell exactly what it was and it was beginning to make him very nervous. The Queen could also feel it too but she had a job to weave enough stories around the young lad so he can't tell the difference between the truth and a lie. The Queen tells her son, "Are you finding things here to your liking? Has everyone treated you well my son? I can also see that you are very uneasy about being around me but that is only because that is what the Scar wanted. He wanted to keep us divided to keep us from uniting."

The Queen continues, "Because if we unite the world will never know what hit them. We have everything we need now to take control of the world before the titan can finish his plans." Mid-sentience Sebak says, "Titan? What Titan? Scar never said anything about a titan being my enemy." She explains, "There is a chaos titan that cannot be named. I will not utter it you because you are not ready to fight such a creature. This Titan is to bring something that everyone fears to this day. He is the one that will bring Ragnarök to us all. He is not the only issue at hand as of right now. The demon Malborh has tricked you, my son." Sebak's eyes did not know what she was talking about. "Yes, my son there are many planning against you. Sooner or later the walls will close in on you, my son. What will you do when everyone is against you and it is only you left standing?"

Sebak answers with a little anger, "I will fight to my last breath for those I love. Your words will not sway me to join you mother I will not kill my friends." Before he could finish his words, the Queen tells him, "What if I could tell you that the Amazons were all under a spell? A spell that I ordered them to be put under." He responds, "Why would you do that?" She continues, "Because I wanted time with you, my son. Time that everyone was taking from us. During this time, I have learned something worse. The very woman you love is the key to everything. She is far more powerful than you will ever be on your own. She is the key to bringing the Titan here to our world. We must kill her now. before anyone else learns of this."

The conversation took a different turn very quickly for the two of them. Because Sebak did not like what he was hearing coming out of his mother's mouth. He was almost ready to fight his own mother. When he put his hand down to his side, he realized that he no longer has his weapons with him. The Queen says, "Was that a threat my son?" soldiers that were outside the room come charging into the throne room and pointing their weapons as Sebak.

The Queen stands up and informs her son, "You will

learn how things really work my son." She signals the men to attack Sebak. The soldiers put down their weapons and jumps Sebak. Sebak puts up a fight but he is outnumbered and outplayed by his own mother. Then the Queen continues, "I have risked everything to make my kingdom great. I will not let your honor stop me from creating the dream that I have waited a thousand years for. When the Amazonians come to take our kingdom and they will. I want you to not hesitate to kill that key. Or the entire world will be destroyed because of your feelings." The blows stop on Sebak when his mother crouches next to him. "Now my son… Are you onboard? Or do I have to discipline you further?"

Sebak spits out a little blood and stares his mother in the eyes and tells her, "I will never betray those that I love. I promised myself that I would never be like my father or like you. I will end this cycle of hatred that has gone on for too long. If I have to give the very shirt off of my back for someone I would do it. My honor is what keeps me going. You can beat my body but I will always…" he begins to stand up as he says these words. "Always… Rise again." The soldiers drop their weapons and bow to Sebak for forgiveness against the Queen's wishes. She turns to see her soldiers bowing to her son after the speech and she did not know how to retaliate to him.

She tells them all, "Get out… Get out!" Sebak stares her down as he walks out of the room. The soldiers run away in fear from the throne room. She could not believe her eyes what was happening. Her son has been a man for a while and he is beginning to rise against her. She begins to cry a little because she knows what must be done now. She Says to herself, "I wanted my son to help me unite our race. It looks like I will have to do it all alone. I tried to be the loving mother. Now I must be the queen from hence forth. Rebellion is imminent now more than ever. My son will eventually become the head of the very snake that I will have to destroy."

On Sebak's side of things once walking out of the throne room the soldiers ask Sebak for his forgiveness. Many of the people bow to Sebak because it was a moment that was told to everyone. He was beaten down by multiple soldiers and he stood up without a limp or a hint of anger towards the soldiers. He knew that they were doing what the queen asked and nothing more. Before he knew it all of the people in the kingdom were bowing before him. The Queen looks down from her balcony and sees her son being bowed to by all of the people. The sight was a surprising moment to them all. She did not know what to do with the situation. Things were starting to unfold really quickly and not in the Queen's favor.

But one thing did get accomplished that she was hoping for to happen in her lifetime. Their people were starting to unite once and for all. The Nagas have been divided for centuries and because of that they have been in the shadows away from everyone else. Sebak may have changed everything for her. But in the end, she may or may not be the head of the snake by the end. But either way her goals may be completed. She didn't want to send the guards after them because that would not look good for anyone. He is the prince of the Nagas after all. It is only right that he is bowed to by those that are lower than him. The people did not see themselves as lower than Sebak though, they could see him as their deliverer from evil.

The Queen smirked a little at what she was seeing and began to draw out her new plans for her people. In one way or another she will get to see the change that her people need in their lives. The plan to gain her son's allegiance has not entirely failed completely. Now she uses her magic mirror to communicate with her spy on the Amazonian Island. They were to step up their plans because of the way things were unfolding with Sebak and the Queen's people. She tells her spy, "Commence with the spell on the Key. If we can get them to attack us, we will be able to unite the Naga race once and for all. In the end he won't make a difference. I am."

CHAPTER 12: UNKNOWN POTENTIAL

Meanwhile, Neville Khan and his people return to their ancestral lands along with many of the other tribes. Everyone gathered near their sacred temple that is hidden with nature magic. Every clan setup their own camps and they all greeted one another. But there was a little dissention between some of the Khans and Neville. Because they heard of how the previous Khan of the clan had fallen. But they did not express their disgust just yet because they had been summoned here for a reason. Everyone showed the druids the utmost respect when being summoned by them. Being summoned by the Circle of the Druids is an honor that is rare for many Khans. None understood why they all were being summoned now at this point in time. This is the biggest summoning ever in their history that they know of.

"Welcome all for the has summoned you here." The druids say in unison. Everyone showed respect to the druids by being completely quiet when they were talking. "There is a matter that must be handled and addressed. Thy is a druid among you. Thy must be revealed and answer the call to the All Mother." Says the druids. Everyone was in shock when the druids told them that there is a potential druid among them and they didn't know it. Neville started to get a little nervous because he could feel that it was him, they were looking for. During the battle with that wizard, he felt the hand of the All Mother. But he was not fully sure. It was when he was knocked unconscious was when adrenaline was very high.

He also knew that some did not agree with him being the new Khan so easily and wanted to challenge him for the right of being the Khan. He was in a very difficult situation and did not know how to deal with it all at once. But out of respect for their culture he knew what he must do even if it was to put a target upon his back from this moment forth. Before everyone began to talk before the Druids asked to valuate everyone of the Khans. Neville begins to step forward.

The Khans were surprised that he stepped forward to the druids without hesitation. They all began to smirk a little at the little boy stepping up to the druids. They did not believe that he of all people the runt of the litter would ever be a druid. When the Khans began to laugh at Neville someone stepped out of the group of Druids that made a hush come over everyone at the temple. It was Elurian the elf that was at the battle of the tribes. Everyone was in aww and amazement at the presence of Elurian. "Yes, you are the one young one. I am glad you have stepped forward." Everyone bows to the druids and Elurian because they are in the presence of greatness for their clan. This will likely never happen again in their time. Neville's mother did not understand what was happening but she did understand their traditions.

The druids surround Neville and they could sense some magical presence about him. they could sense a strong connection to the All Mother and they were astonished that such a connection existed and that they let it get passed them at his birth. "We did not sense this before. Thy has a powerful connection to the All Mother. How did we not know this?" the Druids says to one another. Elurian answers them, "Because Phyrra and I did not deem it so. We wanted a druid that really could understand every aspect of the world. Because for what is to come, we need uniqueness not a follower." The druids were a little confused about what Elurian was trying to tell them. Elurian dismisses everyone but the druids and Neville from the temple.

Elurian tells Neville, "You have a huge choice to make son. You have just recently been making the Khan of your clan. But you also at the same time showed the All Mother who you really are while you were unconscious. She began to heal you before you even received any type of help. Meaning that you are one of her chosen. More so than any of the Druids standing here. You don't have to decide now young one. But the decision will have to be made or it will be taken out of your hands. We will give you two days to decide your fate my son."

The Druids and Elurian begin to walk back into the temple and leave Neville to his thoughts. Before they could leave his sight, Neville says, "Wait..." they turn around when he begins to speak to them. "I do not know much about leading people and I don't know anything about the sacrifices that a Khan must make to see his people through. I know that role has never been for me. I do not know how to take on those kinds of struggles. But to help nature and the world prevent evil from showing it's face ever again. I can do that. I know how to do that." Elurian smirks a little at the young man and was surprised that he decided so quickly.

He says to him, "I am surprised you have come to this conclusion so quickly. Most would take their time to process the situation. You know what you are giving up correct? This choice means that you will now be a shepherd of the world and protect jungles and other types of forests from the potent evil that plagues our world. You would have to denounce your clan and your families to travel the world alone and do as the All Mother tells you." Neville understood what he was agreeing to. He tells Elurian, "I know you don't have to give me a chance to back out. I am ready for what I have chosen to do with my life. I do not want anyone else to suffer when I could have stopped the evil before it showed its face."

Elurian did not think that the humans could surprise him any more than they already have. But this one brought a small smile to his face. He reminded him of a human he once knew in his past life. They take him deeper into the temple to begin the ceremony and one of the druids informs his clan that he has chosen to become a druid over being a Khan. Meaning that they would have to discuss among themselves to find their new Khan. Neville's mother was proud of her son to make the right decision for him. Meaning that she knew what she must do for the clan from now on. Inside the temple Neville had to shed all of his possessions from his past to become one with the All Mother and become one of her druids.

Neville and the druids would go far under the sacred temple a place that only the druids could go. As they descended into the earth to start his druid journey, they had him shed all of his earthly materials on his body. When they arrived at their destination, Neville could see the roots of the world tree and how everything was connected through these roots and they led to a huge pond of glowing water. He only partly understood what was happening and guessed that they were about to put him in the pool of water. The druid escorting him to the pool informs him, "Every one of our temples are sacred they have been here since the dawn of time. Each one of them is connected to the flow of the All Mother herself." Neville was in aww by what he was seeing around him, while listening to the druid.

"Everything you see here comes from the All Mother. She created this world and she can end it any time she chooses. They do not call her Mother Nature for no reason. You are about to give your entire life and being to her and her alone. You will not be able to father children or ever get married. Is that understood young one?" Neville agrees to the terms without knowing what he was giving up. In his head, "I know I have never really felt the warmth of a woman but it will be worth giving up to save the people I love and to earn my place in this world. I do not want to be known as the man that only followed his traditions but also helped deliver the world from evil." Neville shed his clothes as he stood next to the pool and gazed into the glowing water.

The Druids tells him, "Young one… This will be a spiritual journey. One you must take alone. We will stay here to watch over your body. But the journey is for you alone. It will only be you, your demons, and the All Mother. If she rejects you, you will wake in a field as if you had never been here. If she accepts you then she will tattoo your body with runes and give you a gift of your own spiritual making. Step into the pool at your own lesser."

Neville steps into the pool and submerges himself entirely to the water. Once he was inside the water his soul was taken from his body as his body sank to the bottom of the pool. Putting him a comma like state but he was still able to breath underwater do the pool's magic. When he opens his eyes there was nothing but a vast ocean and not thing but the open sky as far as the eye could see. He did not understand what was going on at first. He looked down and saw that he was floating in midair. He was unable to touch the water or anything in the area. When he looks around the landscape would change to different things. All things that he enjoyed deep in his subconscious. The confusion was all in his mind and he needed to calm down. Once he discovered that everything was changing because of him, he calmed himself.

Once he was calm again the terrain turned back into a beach and he was able to touch the sand this time. A soothing but booming voice from behind him says, "I was wondering if you going to be able to calm down on your own." Neville turns around to discover who the All Mother is. When he turns his eyes lay on a beautifully blue scaled dragon with sapphire eyes. She was not the largest dragon recorded in history of them. But she was one of the first ever dragons to walk the earth in the time of the dragons. He knew exactly who she was and did not flinch at the sight of her. He felt very calm and relieved that the All Mother was her. He says, "I did not know you were the All Mother. I'm a little pleased that it is you. My mother would tell me stories about you."

The All Mother informs him, "This is not my true form. I take this form because it brings you comfort. I am not the dragon the call Phyrra. She is one of my daughters. One that is a direct descendant of mine. We are not here to discuss her young one. We are here to discuss you and what you truly want to be. You have many outcomes my dear child. But it is for you to decide what you become no one can tell you who you want to be. The path is always laid before you."

"You have always let the wind and waves carry you young one. You have never been tied down to one place and never let your heritage stop you from exploring and learning of the world. you have led a life of piracy and of a ranger. You have done many things to survive and I would not fault you for that. But you have also done many questionable things. Things that if your parents knew they would be ashamed of you. You must deal with your own guilt if you are to move forward. It will show me your true character and what you are to become once you are a druid. Becoming a druid is no easy feat under me. I have two types of druids; the religious ones and the guardians. Which will you become my son?"

Neville was left alone with his thoughts alone the very mental ideas that haunt him to this day. The terrain around him started to spin around him and it seemed as though his spirit was being pulled apart. He could see many dimensions and he was falling through them all. He did not know what he has put himself into. It seemed as though he was falling forever until he finally stopped and hit the ground. Images began to play in his head, the images that has haunted him for many years. The images that keep him up at night and have him regretting his choices and his path in life. He could hear voices saying, "What makes you think you are worthy?" he did not answer any of the voices and watched the images unfold. He watched as he once helped pirates raid ships and hurt many people.

The voices would go on to say, "What gives you the right? Why would you hurt innocent people?" He looked on as he stood by as his captain executed innocent people because they were rich. He watched as the pirates' burned homes that were alone the beaches because they thought it was funny for them to hurt people that have worked hard for a living. Neville did not agree with everything that the captain did. He would turn his head when something evil was done to someone innocent. He realized what was happening to him at this moment.

The spirits of the past druids are tormenting him because they believe that he is not worthy of such an honor. He was starting to see why so many do not become druids because many people cannot see past their own guilt. They cannot see past their own turmoil that they do not see or remember the good that they have accomplished or the good they did in a bad situation. Neville finally answers the voices, "You want me to fail. I will NOT! You are trying to get me to back down and fell insecure about myself and my choices. Yes, I have done regrettable things. But I have also seen amazing things and done good as well. I had to wear a mask and hide who I am for most of my life. I'm a man and the world does not accept our feeling and our emotions."

"I have been in world where I had to hide my heart and what I believed. A male cannot break down in front of anyone because the world would see him as weak. If I never was in that life, I would not know about the evil that plagues this world. There have been many times that I have looked at my own reflection and wondered why am I here. But I have kept going on matter what I have seen or done. You point out the bad, well let me point out the good. Yes, I was there when my captain did something horrible because he felt that he could. I was also the only man to step up and say something when he was in the wrong. I would get beaten down by his crew for speaking against him many times."

All the druids of the past began to pay attention to Neville as he spoke back to them. The All Mother was proud of what she was seeing. She knew what would happen when Neville was backed into a corner by them. She wanted to see if he was still the man, she has watched all this time grow up. Neville continued, "You have to be in the world to understand it. Hiding away in temples will not help the world. I ask myself every day that I grab my weapons; What a warrior will do? Am I loyal, brave, and True to myself? Who am I without my armor?"

Back in the real world the druids felt a strong magical presence in front of them. The magical prowess surprised them as they only felt this level of magic in a celestial or a dragon. Neville shot out of the pool unconscious and was floating above them. He was the first to ever do that after leaving the pool of magic. His entire body was magically covered in runes and his eyes glowed upon them opening a yellow color. Meaning that he is to be a guardian druid and they bowed to the All-Mother's decision. He was also magically clothed in loose-fitting pants for high kicks, a black undertunic, and a black cloak. He levitated to the ground and once he touched the ground with his feet he was blessed with a root of the eternal tree. Meaning he could use it in any way he chose.

Once he was finished with his druid trial, Elurian returned to take Neville on pilgrimage they would call it. But he did not want to leave without saying goodbye to his mother. When he returned to the surface with Elurian, he discovered that he had been down there for a day. Many rituals have been done sense he left his people's sight. Once they all laid eyes on him, they immediately bowed to his presence and Elurian's. Neville walked straight to his mother and he learns that she is the new Khan of their clan. The first ever female Khan of history. Elurian says, "It seems as though your family loves breaking barriers. I love seeing a good change in the world." he smiles a little at seeing her crown.

He hugs his mother and says, "None of this would be possible without you mother. I love you. Thank you for giving me the chance to prove myself." She responds, "Nonsense I always knew you were worthy of anything you set your mind to. I will always have your back my son. I am always proud of you." Neville smiles at his mother and was happy to hear what she said. He now focused on the task as hand being his pilgrimage. Elurian asked Neville, "Are you ready?" and Neville nods at him. the portal opens and they step through while his mother drops a tear.

CHAPTER 13 THE EVIL WITHIN

After a few days passed, The Queen brings her son outside their castle walls to show him something important. She shows him all those that have died under the rule of man and how war is all they understand. Sebak was getting tired of hearing about war from her and did not want to listen to her talk about it anymore. *"I don't want to hear this anymore mother. I am at peace. Let's leave it at that."* He says to her. She responds, *"How does this not make you angry? How can you be this way and be my child?"* he responds, *"Who taught you how to hate? All this hate coming from you, it is not who you are. Hate is taught not born. What brought all this hate to you? That is what I want to talk about. Otherwise, I do not want to hear of the subject anymore."* Sebak begins to walk back to the castle without his mother.

She stops and thinks about what has happened to her and why is she so hateful. She started to look inwards because of her child. She tells Neville before he is too far away, *"It was your father. He taught me how to hate humanity. despite him also being a human himself. When he introduced himself, he was what a human would call the perfect person. He was sweet to me in every way. Something a human would call a gentleman. He was what I was looking for in a husband, but the Naga race does not believe in marriage because we all mate. He made me feel special. Until one day something changed inside him. the man I once loved was completely gone. Yes, I played my mind games with him before, but this was different. He had turned to the dark side. This happened when I was ready to give birth to you, my son."*

Sebak turns to his mother to listen to her and watch to see if she is lying to him. She continues, *"Later, your father returned to our castle with unbelievable power. Granted I did not give him any other choice I was manipulating him when he first started out his journey. I do admit that. But I have run a kingdom for so long what a girl to do when it comes to fun."*

"He had discovered what I have done to him and the people he said he loved. He also learned the truth about how the Nagas work in their culture. How they are made to manipulate the ones they love or the ones they want. At the time I had four children that have become princess in the eyes of the kingdom. He did not like how I ruled here and how everything was so twisted. He decided to overthrow me. I was not going to take his challenge lying down. We fought for a long time. My children jumped to defend their mother at her weakest point. Fighting a man that I loved and a man that I wanted to rule by my side. He decides to usurp me. We told the children not to interfere but they were grown."

"Your father is the reason some of our customs have changed to keep something like that from happening again so easily. During the fighting he killed all of my children that I actually claimed. Even in my rage I could not stop him. he killed them in front of me brutally and beat the fight out of me. he then stood over me and told me that he wasn't going to kill me. He was going to make me watch as he changed my world. Destroy it if he needed to and then I would have his permission to die. He put me in the dungeons to watch as things around me changed and I had no hand in any of it. Instead of putting the crown on his head he put it on Scar's wife's head instead. I do not remember her name because I

kill those that I remember that have wronged me."

"Your father was a hero Sebak I don't deny that. But he was a villain to some as well. He was a good man at heart but he did some horrible things to make change happen. He put that woman on the throne and she created peace among the Naga clans and united them under the kingdom. Together they all would go on to fight the very evil that corrupted Bakari. The demon that you trusted in the beginning of your journey. The old man that said he posed as someone that was close to you. Mal… which his real name is Malborh, but you already know that."

Sebak did not like all that he heard but he could tell it was all the truth from her body language. He did not know what to say to his mother because it seemed to take everything for her to actually open up to her son. She was beginning to cry and did not want to show her son her tears. He could see the regret and the remorse that was in her eyes. He could not see any manipulation tactic here at all. It was purely her being vulnerable in front of her son. Something she never shows in front of anyone is her weakness. All that she has been through and she has always wanted to play the role of a warrior like everyone else. He breaks and hugs his mother because it felt like to him that she needed one. He tells his mother, *"Its alright mother. I understand that everyone makes mistakes in the spar of the moment."*

The two of them could speak to one another openly while they were outside the castle. They could finally be mother and son and not a Queen and a prince. The queen could finally be Minerva once again. *"You both were in the wrong mother. From what you tell me and what Scar has told me. he was being tugged in multiple directions because of the way the world is. He was loyal to the cause. But the trouble with that is that the cause will always betray you. A person cannot get lost in that. Getting lost in what you must do and not taking a moment to be weak around your family and friends. A recipe for disaster and the trauma could have done many things to my father's mind. I would not wish that on anyone. Our family needs to seek redemption. I myself need to seek it for our family considering my father is no longer here to do so."*

"I need to see Scar one last time, I am sure that he knows more about my father than anyone. He was his right hand; Scar would tell me how he was always with him. I must go see him and then I will make up my decision on how to proceed mother. But annihilating the humans is not the answer. There is always another way. The people in my life have taught me that."

Meanwhile, Neville and Elurian could feel a pull through their magic. Their magic led them to the Amazonians once again. The Amazonians attempted to attack them for them trespassing. Their magic told them that there was a massive spell that has been used on them all. It was a very powerful mind control spell that was also difficult to detect even by the strongest of magic users. It was a very easy spell that can be used over time with an artifact. Elurian and Neville did not want to attack the young women trying to defend their home. Elurian tells Neville to locate the source of the spell while he dispelled the Amazonians. Once upon getting most of the Amazonians to attack Elurian he was able to dispel the magic that was controlling them before they could injure him.

Dispelling the magic revealed where the magic was

coming from in an instant. The magic was coming from a necklace upon one of the Amazonians. The Queen of the Amazonians informed Elurian, *"Thank you for releasing us. We are eternally in your debt."* Once the they discovered where the spell was coming from. The Queen informs the two of them, *"That is not once of our Amazonians."* Elurian and Neville both tried to catch her after the queen informed them. It took a second for the two of them to catch her because she was trained like an Amazonian. But they women of the island were the ones to catch her. Not wanting to be in debt to men for long they ended that quickly.

She informs the two of them, *"This chameleon will face Amazonian justice. And we will interrogate her on how she was able to use the spell so widely on all of them at the same time. We will inform you of what we find and then you can be on your way."* The Chameleon did nothing but laugh as she was being dragged away. She says, *"You may have stopped me. but you will not stop her. You saved these warriors but you cannot stop the princess."* She laughs maniacally before the doors closed. Neville's eyes grew very wide as he the realization set in.

Back at Khuvia, Minerva and Sebak have talked things over and she began to calm down about destroying humanity. She started to act like a mother to Sebak for the first time. Everyone began to see a change in the queen. It was a change that the entire civilization could appreciate. They all knew that Sebak was what they needed to change things around here because the Queen would not listen to anyone around here. But they knew the son that she created with the man she loved would be able to change her cold heart. There was a certain change in the wind all of sudden around the kingdom. Soldiers were running to protect the castle without orders. None knew what was going on. Sebak stops a solider and asked, *"What is happening around here?"*

The Soldier responds, *"There is a threat outside the gates. It seems to be a very skilled warrior. They are cutting down our people. Its some sort of an attack on us. We are going to defend the castle."* Sebak looks up in the direction of the soldiers running. He responds, *"Do not leave the walls I will deal with the situation."* He goes to intercept the reinforcement soldiers to stop any more lives being taken. He runs through the gates and into the forest after the soldiers. Once in the forest and arriving at the location of the attackers. He discovers something he thought he would never see. There was carnage everywhere in the forest. Trees broken down soldiers laying deceased on the ground brutally.

In the center of it all was a woman that he recognized from first glance. It was the woman he loved with all his heart and soul. The woman he risked his life and an entire battle to save. He watched in disgust and confusion. He says, *"Alessia what… what are you doing?"* as she finishes off the last soldier, she looks at Sebak like she did not even know who he was and started walking towards him. Sebak asks her, *"Who did this to you?"* as she charges him. He manages to block the punch that she through at him. He could tell she was using full force on him. He could also tell that she did not recognize him in any way.

He did not know what to think of this situation as he was flying back from the force of the punch. He catches himself and begins to recover from the attack but Alessia hits him once again and this one was off-guard. He says after catching his breath and tumbling a few times, *"Really? Sucker punch? That is below you. Who are you and what have you done with my Alessia?"* the two would begin to battle with Sebak on the receiving end of all the attacks. He did not want to hurt Alessia no matter what was happening with her. He ends up tumbling out in the open in front of the Khuvia. Alessia was like a mad monster on a rampage. The civilians and the soldiers looked on with concern for their prince.

The soldiers began to aim their bows and crossbows at Alessia. Sebak says, *"NO! DO NOT FIRE A SINGLE SHOT!"* as he tussles with Alessia. *"She is someone very important to me. you will not harm her no matter what she does to me."* The two seemed to be even fighting. But Sebak was holding back out of fear of hurting Alessia. He did not know if he could help her and protect the people within the castle walls. He would eventually have to stop pulling his punches or it could cost lives. A choice he was needing to make and it was needing to be made quickly as she was pushing the fight closer and closer to the castle.

He started matching her punching power to protect the castle behind him. He started to master his anger and use his strength to his advantage. The only thing on Alessia that he noticed was new were the gauntlets that she was wearing. Every time they matched punches the gauntlets would crack. Once there was enough damage to the gauntlets Alessia started to wake up. She said, *"What? Where am I?"* and then she noticed that she was fighting Sebak. *"Sebak what are you doing her? Why are you sparing with me?"* Sebak Answers her, *"We aren't sparing you seem to be trying to kill me. my dear."* She did not like the answer and said,

"What? I would never do that. I..." and then she snapped back to the monster the gauntlets want her to be.

The fight went on and the monster raged within Alessia and she began to slam Sebak around her. He did not want to hit her in any way possible if he could help it. He would defend himself, but he would not hurt her. Between protecting the people and protecting her he knew what he would choose in a heartbeat. The monster raged from deep within her and he could sense this somehow. He did not want to keep fighting someone he loved so dearly. He started to run out of ideas on how to protect both her and the castle. He had one last idea and he told himself, *"If this doesn't work then I do not know what will. But I'll do anything for Alessia."* He stopped fighting her and put his hands down.

Everyone looked on as Alessia began to beat down Sebak. She would hit him and he would stand back up. He tells her, *"I Know you are in there Alessia. After all we have been though. Your goanna let a couple of gauntlets beat you? No. you are a warrior. A warrior that the world can be proud of."* She continued to hit him to the point that he was beginning to spit up blood. But he kept getting back up no matter what. He continued, *"If you want to kill me that is fine. I won't stop you if that is what you wish. I am with you to the end of the line Alessia."* She hits him some more and this time he could not get up on his own anymore. But he was still moving and being defiant to her no matter what.

Alessia begins to go for the killing blows on Sebak. The soldiers began to ready their aim to fire upon Alessia at the behest of the Queen. Alessia was already fighting the monster on the inside. She was holding back a lot of power in many of those punches. For the killing blow she began to miss her shots. She did not want to kill the man she loved. She was fighting with everything in her to fight back to the surface. Sebak tells her, *"I don't care what others think about you. I love you. I love you more than life itself. My life is nothing if it means that I can save you."* Alessia misses the attack again and he takes the opportunity to kiss Alessia.

The kiss from the man she loves dearly began to snap her out of the spell. She begins pulling on the gauntlets and trying to take them off of her. The Queen was surprised by what was happening down there. She did not know he loved her that much and she did not know that the young woman loved him back. Their love was strong enough already that she was capable of fighting off a mind control spell. Alessia manages to break off the left gauntlet because of how damaged it was. It was the right one that would not break easily. It seemed once one of them had been destroyed the other became stronger. Alessia was down on her knees and yelled as she pulled the right gauntlet off of her arm.

Once she pulled it off a shock way went over the area and she was knocked unconscious. Sebak sits up a little as he was already beginning to heal from his injuries. The first thing he does is crawl to Alessia to see if she was alright. She awakens to him laying next to her and smiling in her face. A sight she often dreamed of actually happening one day but she did not want to admit it to herself. She smiled a little and blushed at the sight of seeing his face upon waking up. Even if it was from her being unconscious. She did not know what to say to him at all until she looked down at her hands. The blood all over her hands shocked her and knocked her out of her day dream.

She began to hyperventilate from what she had done

while under the influence of that spell. She began to shake and did not know what to do with herself. Sebak sat up next to her as she was trembling and decides to hold her. She did not understand as to why he would do that after what she has done. He tells her, *"It was not you. It was not the real you. I know the real you. You would never do something like that. You do not have to talk about it. Just know I am here."* She did not know how to respond to Sebak's words. She sat there shaking and thinking about what she had done. She finally stopped shaking because of Sebak's comforting.

Arriving after the fight were the two that were dealing with the Amazonians, Elurian and Neville. Making sure all of the Amazonians were no longer under the spell before arriving to assist Sebak with Alessia. Sebak looks up to see them arrive through a portal as the soldiers are also running towards them. He says, *"Oh better late than never I suppose!"* Neville responds, *"No need for your sarcasm Sebak we were dealing with a threat on the Amazonian Island. There was a mole there that was employed by."* Before he could finish his sentence, the Queen arrived with some soldiers. The Queen says, *"Arrest her."* But Sebak stops the soldiers as he started to stand up. He says, *"I will not allow her to be arrested mother. I know what is going on already."* She looked confused by her son and did not understand.

Before anyone could say anything to Sebak he already knew what this was about. He sends the guards back to the castle because no one would be getting arrested. He says to her after the soldiers left ear shot, *"She only attacked the castle as a last-ditch effort for you to turn me against humanity. I figured it out as I was fighting her. Because I know Alessia better than you think."* Elurian and Neville move away from them to talk to Alessia and comfort her. Sebak tells his mother, *"We are through. I thought there was some sort of compassion within you but I was wrong. I cannot help you mother. You need to learn that all of humanity is not horrible. Some of the damage to your soul was done to yourself. Take responsibility for your own actions."*

After Sebak talks to his mother he walks over to Alessia to see if she was alright. Neville and Elurian did not know what to do because of what they talked about with Alessia. They did not have a right to interfere because it was her decision. Before Sebak could say anything Alessia says, *"I'm leaving Sebak. There is no reason to stop me. I have done horrible things here that I need to atone for. I also need to find myself and understand who I want to be in this world. I cannot do that with you and I having conflicting feeling about one another. I can't, goodbye."*

Alessia says this to him while her back is turned to him because she could not look him in the eye and say this to him. He did not know what to say to her and she would not allow him to get the chance to say anything to her. She decides to walk away from both her friends and family along with the Amazonians. It was a difficult decision to make but she felt as though she needed to make that decision. Sebak did not know what to do or say because he did not want her to go. He tries to go after her but Neville stops him. both of them were hurting because this entire journey they have been together except for the past few months. Everything started once the three of them were together.

With everything over with Elurian and Neville had to

leave as well. But Neville had to make sure that Sebak was okay. *"Are you okay brother? I know it hurts. But you have to let her figure out what she wants in life."* Sebak looking in the direction that she walked away in and watching the sun go down. He says, *"I know. I just have this feeling that I will never see her again."* Neville pats Sebak's shoulder to comfort him. He turns around to hug his friend Neville. Sebak tells Neville, *"Be safe my brother."* Neville responds, *"Always you know me."* he says with a smile and a light chuckle. Neville asks him, *"What are you going to do?"* he responds, *"I'm going to see Scar. I have a few questions for him. then I will try to find myself with all the time I have."* He says with a smirk and a light chuckle as well.

"Alright brother I know how to find you. I will be checking on you." Neville says before leaving through a portal. *"I'm sure you will my friend. I'm sure you will."* Sebak says to himself. He goes to his room in the castle and packs what he needs and tells his mother goodbye. He did not want to hold anything against her. It was no reason to do so because she and his father has done the damage. Before he leaves, he tells her, *"No one can heal your pain but yourself. You need to forgive him mother and move on with your life. Or your life will pass you by."*

For five weeks Sebak traveled alone to find his old mentor Scar. He remembered what they once talked about he would go once he could be with his family. It took him a month to find where he had gone. When he makes it to the place, he finds four children running around playing and two large snakes watching the house. The children were playing tag with one another and having fun. Nyssa walked out the front door because she could see him from the window. The children stopped playing for a second because they wanted to know who he was. Nyssa tells the children, *"Its alright children. It's a friend. Go play."* She walks towards Sebak and gives him a hug. The children go back to playing and continue to run around the field. Sebak smiled as he could see such peace in one place.

Nyssa says, *"Hello Sebak how are you?"* He answers, *"I'm good. I could be better. But I'm good. I love your home. You and Scar have done well for yourselves. I'm happy for you both."* He says with a smile. Nyssa tells him, *"Yes well Scar insisted that he build it from the ground up. He said we would appreciate it more. And by God that man was right."* She laughs and says, *"Don't tell him I said that."* The both of them look at this amazing home built out of brick and wood. Nyssa says, *"It took us a while but we built the house together. I love everything about it. I don't regret giving up the life we had for this. Come on I'll show you where he is."*

They walk through the house and Sebak sees beautifully built home within. It had wooden floor in certain parts of the house and a marble floor as well. They had many vases with flowers with them around the house. From the look of the house, they did entirely leave their past behind them. He thought to himself, *"Then it is possible to leave the war and all the bloodshed."* They walk to the back of the house and he sees Scar in the back of the house at his self-built forge. He had everything he needed to build a house and more if needed. Nyssa says, *"Hey honey there is someone here to see you."*

Scar was surprised to see Sebak and wondered what was wrong immediately. Scar says, *"Hello young man. look at you. Ur scared up as much as I am almost."* He says with a light laugh. Nyssa says, *"I am going to go get you two something to drink. Sebak, you look like you need one."* As she walks away. *"What is wrong? Young one. You only have that face when something is bothering you."* Sebak tried to deny that something was wrong by saying, "Nothing I just wanted to see my mentor." He looks at him with an eyebrow raised and he says, *"Right."* with a little sarcasm. He tells him, *"Sit down I would love to know what is going on with you. I do want to get one thing off my chest first. I am sorry we left you with all that to deal with my boy. I just could not deal with all the bloodshed anymore."*

Before he could finish talking Sebak says, *"It is okay mentor. I understand. You have a family to think about. You have nothing to be sorry for. I am fine mentor. We all have been through a lot."* He tells Scar the entire story of what has happened the past few months and the entire thing shocked him. He did not know what to tell Sebak right off the top. He did not have the words to describe anything. He did not know what to say exactly. Scar says, *"I'm sorry you had to go through that alone my boy. I should not have left your side."* Sebak replies, *"It is okay mentor. Like I said before. You had to do what was right for your family. I had to do what was right for me. I thought my mother could change. But she would not her hate has a strong hold over her."*

Scar then says, *"Pore Alessia as well. She has something that no one else can help but herself. She is dealing with the pain of knowing she has hurt innocent people. Only she can rise out of that hole on her own. Do not blame yourself Sebak. She needs to do this alone. Finding peace is grueling, it is a fight to the death, the defeat of evil and maliciousness within."* Sebak huffed to himself after Scar said that. He then says, *"You always know what to say mentor."*

Scar could see that Sebak was struggling within himself as well. He tells the young one, *"Maybe it is time that you learned how you are."* Sebak started to think to himself and says, *"Yes. I do need to focus on myself. Learn something that can keep my attention. Keep my mind clear of doubt."* Scar says, *"Yes that is what you need."* Then Sebak asks him, *"Then could you teach me the Flash Step?"* Scar was shocked by him asking that and he looks him in the eye before answering that question. He looked deep into Sebak's eyes and he could see something. Scar asks him, *"Why do you want to know the Flash Step?"* He answers, *"Because it is something I watched you do. It seems to take a lot of discipline to master such a move. I also love martial arts. I thought to ask that sense we were talking about me learning who I am. If anything, the training would help me learn more about myself."*

Scar says, *"The Flash Step will not tell you anything about yourself. That is not who you are."* Sebak was confused by what his mentor just said to him. He goes to say, "What do you mean?" Scar did not want to tell him what he was about to say. But he needed to know and maybe it would save him. He tells Sebak, *"Son there is something I have to tell you. I have had to keep this from you the entire time because I promised."* Sebak was left in suspense and wanted to know what he was talking about.

Scar continues, *"You are more like your father than you realize. You have his magical prowess already. You just have to train and learn how to use it. The strength you have is not because you are a combination of a human and a Naga. It is because of your magical power. Your father was powerful with magic and he could do many things with it. You have inherited that and it is a lot stronger than his. I have watched you closely Sebak and you are heading down the same path as he did.*" Sebak did not like what he was hearing from scar and he stands up. He says, *"Your wrong. Thanks for hiding things from me."* And he walks away from Scar.

CHAPTER 14 THE TRUE FACES OF DARKNESS

Meanwhile, Malborh walks into the kingdom of Vanalaos he meets with the emperor. Malborh sees that he had mobilized an army and they were training for future wars to come. *"Well. Well. Well... What have we here? An emperor that seems to be preparing for something."* he says with a sarcastic smirk as he walks into the private court room with the emperor. The emperor was not happy with their arrangement in the slightest. The emperor says, *"Quiet demon! You should learn to hold your tongue when you're talking to royalty."* Malborh picks the emperor up by his throat. *"You should watch who you're talking to. I am the true royalty here. I am the son of your boss. The Titan that holds your leash human."*

In front of them was a magical mirror that showed the face of a titan. Malborh's father says, *"Now son. Do not hurt the help."* Malborh puts the emperor down and he chokes and gasps for air. Malborh says to his father, *"I was only playing father."* Aethos cuts him off, *"I don't need your banter son. I have something important to tell you."* He tells the emperor, *"Leave us."* And the emperor does exactly that on command from the titan. *"Now boy! It is time to put our plans into full motion. I can feel the change in the wind. You have done well breaking the heroes. Did you find the key?"* Malborh answers, *"Yes father. It is inside the body of a human. Of all the humans it is inside a woman by the name of Alessia. I could not get to the key without blowing my cover."*

Aethos, *"Good. At least we know where to find the key. We will retrieve it in time. Have you gotten the Queen of the Nagas to join our cause?"* Malborh tells him, *"No. she will not join without her son at her side."* He replies, *"Then we will have to work with her successor. Get rid of the ant for me."* Malborh says, *"With pleasure father I have been waiting to do so."* Before he leaves Aethos says, *"And the boy as well."* Malborh nods and teleports away.

While Malborh is on the move he mutters to himself annoyed by his father ordering him around. But he does what he was told because he knows what would happen to him if he did not. He makes it to Khuvia quickly and teleports right into the castle court room. Minerva did not know who was teleporting until he stepped out. She then relaxed because she knew who he was. She says, *"I have not gotten my son to join us just yet. Just give me a little more time. I am sure I can get him to join us."* Malborh walks up to her without saying a word and he asks, *"Were is your son?"* Minerva answers, *"He went hunting. He needed to clear his head."* Malborh says, *"Alright. Then send someone to fetch him. I would like to talk to him myself."*

She then asks, *"Why?"* He answers, *"Because I want him to know I am alright and not dead."* She says, *"Let him be. He is more like his father than I realize. He is stubborn."* Malborh makes a move on Minerva but it was not the real Minerva but a decoy. *"I knew you were here to kill me."* Minerva says as she steps out of the shadows. *"How did you?"* Malborh says. Minerva replies, *"When you stepped out of the portal is when I moved. You gave me time to do so. I did it to see your intentions. You will not lay a hand on my son."* Malborh says, *"Lets talk about this before you get."* He is interrupted midsentence by her snake attacking him. Minerva tells her snake, *"Go find my son and warn him."* the snake goes underground and burrows out of the castle walls to find Sebak.

Malborh smirks and laughs maniacally and says, *"Cleaver and smart move. I am going to enjoy this."* As he cracks his neck. Minerva replies, *"Not as much as I will."* As she shows her true form to Malborh. Her true form consisted of a medusa like form with snakes for hair and a snake tail for legs. The two pulled their weapons and began to clash metal against metal. Minerva tells him, *"You will never get to my son. I will not allow it."* As the two clashed weapons. She even used her tail to attack him as well to keep him off balance.

The two of them began to tear down the castle courtroom. Minerva's soldiers hear the commotion and wanted to help the queen. She says, *"No! evacuate the people. This is my fight you all will only get in the way. Find my son Sebak he is your savior. Do not worry about me. leave while you all can."* The commander says, *"It's been an honor my queen."* And they all run away from the fighting to find the civilians. Minerva would not let Malborh out of her sight buying time for her people to escape the area. At the end of her tail was a blade that she had crafted for herself. She wanted to always have an upper hand against her enemies. Everything around them was beginning to crumble from their tussle.

Malborh tries a few times to get away from Minerva but she was not having it. He was beginning to get tired of her fighting and started to use magic on her. She would not allow him to get off any major spells that would hurt her. But his fire abilities were all he could use at the time. He burned everything around them making a fiery battle to the death. Minerva would try to turn him into stone but it did not work on him because he did not look her in the eyes. He was starting to get very annoyed with her. It seemed as if she has been waiting for this day to come. He could not help also being a little impressed with her.

He figures out how to beat her and waits until she strikes at him with her tail. He manages to use a piece of rubble to trap her tail in place. While she was trying to free her tail, she makes a huge mistake and takes her eyes off of him. He jumps into her face and she could not move quick enough. She attempts to turn him into stone but it was to no avail. He slices her head clean off with one stroke of his blade. Her head tumbles to the floor as does the entire castle. He cleans his blade and says, *"That was a valiant effort on your part. I hope you made peace with yourself."* He laughs. *"Or I will be seeing you very soon once again but as a demon like myself."* He walks away from the ruined castle and sees everyone has gone.

Once Malborh left the ruined castle he felt a presence he had not felt for a long time. A voice behind him says, *"Malborh."* And he turns around to see his rival. Malborh says, *"Elurian."* And he redraws his weapon once again. The two clashes over the rubble with their weapons. When they push off one another they begin using magic to throw fireballs at one another. Elurian says, *"What have you done?"* Malborh laughs and says, *"Late as always elf. Poor Elurian always one step behind me. We will prevail once and for all this time."* As the two fought even harder. The two of them knew each other so well that they knew every move the other would make before they made it.

Elurian says to Malborh, *"Haven't you taken enough from the boy?"* Malborh laughs maniacally and says, *"Not entirely enough he has not snapped like his father did. But he is not who we need anymore. He is only for fun now."* Elurian did not understand what he had in mind. Who could they actually be after if it was not Sebak? The fight was no longer going Malborh's way. Elurian was getting the better of him with his spells. Malborh says, *"So... You can teach an old dog new tricks."* And laughs more. Elurian manages to disarm Malborh and knock him to the ground. Elurian then decides to hold him at sword point and interrogate him. He wanted to know who was so important for them to play with Sebak's emotions.

While he was trying to interrogate Malborh to no avail he was interrupted by an old face. Hiamutt had returned to the planet to assist Malborh in the plan to dominate the world. Hiamutt knocked Elurian to the ground causing him to drop his sword as well. He was not the only face he recognized either. Hiamutt's son Svalgas was also with them as well. Malborh says, *"Outnumbered as always I see."* With a smirk. Another voice says, *"He is not alone."* Phyrra lands behind Elurian after he stand back up and grabs his sword. They were shocked by Phyrra's presence and Malborh says, *"Another time Elurian."* As the three of them teleport away.

Elurian could feel what has happened here and he could not help but feel remorse. *"Late again. What am I to do Phyrra? I always arrive too late. I am never where I need to be."* Elurian says. Phyrra says to him, *"You cannot be in two places at once. You have duties to this world. you tried to respond as quickly as you could. You managed to arrive well before I did. Be happy you were here to even engage him."* Elurian says, *"Its not enough Phyrra I have to stop them. I cannot let this happen for a third time. I failed the boy's father. I cannot fail him too."* Phyrra tells him, *"Then do something different this time."* He did not understand what else he could do differently.

Phyrra tells Elurian, *"Train the boy until he is ready to take on such a threat. Do not allow Malborh to twist the boy's mind entirely. You know you have sensed the magic within him. He is powerful. Possibly more powerful than his father ever could have reached."* He agrees and says, *"Your right Phyrra that would be something Malborh would not expect. But I am no teacher. I have never trained anyone in my entire life. that time with the druid was only guiding him. I was not outright teaching him anything. Everything was already shown to him by the All Mother."* Phyrra says, *"You need to stop doubting yourself. You need to forgive yourself for what you had to do all those years ago."*

Elurian looks into the rubble and sees Minerva's body under the rubble. He thinks how this will affect the boy and his training. He did not know what he should do about this situation and was second guessing the entire situation. He did not want to train Sebak in the mystic arts of magic. With magic Sebak could do anything he wanted. Phyrra says to him, *"You have to give the boy a chance and let him decide who he is going to become. You cannot shield him anymore from what he will become. He is already on the path and you know it as well. It would be better to at least try to guide him in the right direction"* Elurian agrees with Phyrra's argument.

Malborh laughs at Elurian upon their retreat to the castle. *"That elf is so predictable. His time will come. Killing him will be sweeter than honey."* He says while smirking a little and cleaning his blades. Hiamutt and Svalgas shapeshift into their human form to speak to the Titan through the mirror in the castle. The emperor as well was in the room this time as well to learn what their next move will be. When they return to the castle, they give Aethos a full report on what has happened. Aethos was not fully pleased that the boy has eluded Malborh. But he was pleased that an ant was destroyed and out of their way permanently. Aethos tells them, *"Now it is time for the next phase of our plan. We must find the Key and then I can bring my kingdom to the world."*

"I don't care how you do it. Find a way to the key. Find the answer that we need to free me from this retched dimension." Aethos exclaims. The emperor offers his expertise this time for this phase of the plan. He says, *"Instead of risking your heavy hitters let my men do the heavy lifting. Let us do the needless work and discover all you need to know about the key."* Aethos looks at the human and then looks at the other three. He says, *"Go! Oversee this phase. If you complete your task, you will have a place in my new world."* the emperor replies, *"Thank You! Thank you, my lord!"* he says as he bows and leaves the room.

Aethos tells his sons, *"Once the key is found we need to be able to translate the incantation. The quicker I am free. The easier we can turn the world into out world."* Hiamutt says, *"We can finally become world eaters. The highest level of power a demon can achieve."* He says with a sneer.

Svalgas did not care how this went he just wanted to destroy anything in his path. Malborh was ready to remake the world into their image and do whatever they want. *"All this hiding and plotting is exhausting. I cannot wait too finally be free!"* Malborh says.

CHAPTER 15 THE NEW GUARDS

Sebak now decides to go back to the castle of Khuvia because he felt as though there is unfinished business there. While he was traveling, he could feel a disturbance in some way he could feel that something has changed. Then a huge Snake reveals itself from out of the ground. It was his mother's snake and it was distraught for some reason. The snake was very scared and it caught the attention of Sebak's snake. Her snake being there only could mean one thing that his mother was now gone. *"No, it cannot be. This cannot be. What happened? What happened?"* Sebak would say to himself he did not know what to do now. Now he must return to the castle to see what has happened.

The death of Minerva was felt by every Naga even those that were not directly under her rule. The power has finally shifted in a dark direction in the world. Minerva was very misguided but she was also holding the balance between everything as well without knowing it. She was a bridge between chaos and ruin for the Naga races and they all felt it. She had more on her shoulders than any of the other Nagas. Even the changelings could feel her death as it happened. Nyssa and Scar felt her death and instantly knew what has happened in the world. Now they are truly in the endgame of the Titan's plans. All the magic users felt the shift in the magical world.

Sebak had no other choice but to return home and do final rights in their culture. It took him a few weeks to return to Khuvia. The other Nagas returned home as well to bury their queen. But they could not do that until the entire family had returned home. Elurian was not allowed to touch the body even after he helped dig her body out of the rubble. Sebak knew the rules as well because he spent months with them. They could not do anything until they all returned home. A few hours after Sebak showed up Scar also showed up as well. Then they could finally lay Queen Minerva to rest underground. Together they move her to the hall of Kings & Queens burial site.

During the funeral Neville also arrived to support Sebak in his time of need. The entire time the funeral was going on Elurian was reading Sebak and he could tell something was off about the boy. He was taking his mother's death a little too well. But he was going to take Phyrra's advice and try to get him to learn how to use his abilities. He was not going to approach him as of right now though. He was going to allow the young man time to grieve for his mother. After the funeral Sebak approaches Elurian and says, *"You have been paying attention to me the entire day. What is it that you want from me?"* Elurian says, *"I want nothing from you boy. But it is something I can do for you. You have abilities that are hidden and locked away from you. I would like to help you access these abilities."*

Scar over hears what Elurian said to Sebak and could not believe what he was hearing. Scar did not want that for Sebak and he turns around says to them, *"No do not do that Sebak. You will become like your father. Do not do this."* His words caught the attention of everyone in the area. Sebak looks halfway back at Scar and says to Elurian, *"Do not worry I am nothing like my father was."* Elurian takes the boy at his word and the two of them teleport away. Scar did not like that Sebak completely ignored him at that moment.

Scar looks at Neville who did nothing about the situation. He says, "What? It is ultimately his choice just like it was mine to become a druid. Have a little faith in Sebak. He is not as evil as his father was."

"You have not paid attention to your friend then. I can see it in his eyes. He is hurting very badly. Something is hurting him that he does not want to talk about. He won't stay still enough to accept what has happened to him. How are you not worried about your best friend?" Scar says to Neville. Neville replies, *"Because I have faith in my friend that he will stay on the correct path. I will always help him if he needs me and he knows that. I have promised to check on him as much as possible. We both agreed that we would stay communicating."*

Little did they know that Elurian took Sebak somewhere that none were able to find him. Sebak was even confused about where he was at first because he felt trapped. Elurian says to Sebak, *"Here you will train with the High Druids and you will not leave until you get those emotions in order. Also learn some respect for your elders."* Sebak began to grow angry at Elurian for locking him away in a place that he did not know anything about. The High Druids surrounded him and locked him with magical chains and tattooed runes all over Sebak's body. They locked his body down without saying a word or even moving at all. All they did was stand there and locked him into place.

They shave his hair and locked him into a spell that would put him inside his mind. There they would truly test him if he was anything like his father or if he would be a serious problem. Sebak says, *"What is happening where am I?"* a druid enters his mind and says, *"We are in your mind.*

This is where your training will begin my boy." Sebak was confused and didn't know if he wanted this anymore. The Druid says, *"Its too late to turn back now you are here. You might as well learn what you came to learn."* He finally relents and the two of them begin a long vigorous training session. A session that would make Sebak sweat inside his mind and outside his body. The Druids would train him every day and every hour because the fate of the world could one day depend on his shoulders.

The Druids would put him through vigorous training because they knew what could be at stake. They try to train him for every possibility that could happen. but they could not think of every situation. The only thing they were trying to do was to teach Sebak how to survive multiple different situations and stay calm. Through his training his anger was the most emotion to flair up against the druids. They would go on to teach him to control that anger and harness it. Days turned into weeks and weeks turned into months, Sebak was left entirely alone with them.

In those same days Scar wondered if he should return to the fight and not leave Sebak alone anymore. *"Did I make the right decision to walk away from the fighting? I walked away for my family. But did I do it too soon?"* Scar tells himself. Nyssa could see the struggling in Scar's eyes. She wanted to help him any way she could. He stands over a case that was holding his sword inside it. She walks up behind him and holds him from behind. She tells him, *"It is okay dear. Not everything is your fault. Some people have to make their own decisions. You are not responsible for everyone."* Scar goes to say, *"I know I am not responsible for everyone. I promised Bakari on his dying wish to protect his son and guide him. that is the pressure I took when he made me drive a sword through his heart."*

Scar was beginning to break on the inside because he did not truly know exactly what to do. Nyssa says, *"The boy you once knew is now grown my love. He can make his own decisions. You cannot coddle him anymore. Guiding someone through their life does not mean coddling them for their entire life. are you going to be this way with our children?"* she says jokingly. Scar replies to the joke, *"Maybe? I don't know yet their still young."* Making them both laugh. But he could not help but be worried about Sebak and if he left the fight a little too early. Nyssa could tell this would eat at him for a long time until he makes a decision. She goes to say, *"Honey to help easy your mind. Its not your honor that is making you feel torn. It is your pride because you have built your entire life off of your honor. You don't want to see it tarnished."*

Scar looked at her and did not know what to tell her. He could not tell her nothing but the truth. When he finally come clean about the past and how everything went down. Nyssa's eyes opened wide and she did not know what to say to her husband anymore. The only thing she could say was, *"That is awful… I would not wish that guilt upon anyone. I'm sorry my love."* She couldn't do anything but hold her husband after he finally was able to tell someone the truth.

The only time Sebak could leave the tower he was only allowed to visit the neighboring villages. He could see the peace in these villages and how they were untouched by war. Untouched by hate or any of the negative energy and it intrigued him very much. The druids would tell him, *"We felt sorry for some of the villages and decided to protect them from the evil around the world with our magic. Its sad really. Because we cannot shield everyone from evil. Someone really needs to do something about all this hate. There is entirely too much hate in this magical world of ours. It's not just one race with all the pride and hate. All of them has that strong pride and unnecessary hate towards others for no reason. It's all unnecessary to life."*

Sebak said nothing to the druids he was in awe at the beauty of the village that was untouched by war or anything evil. A druid that was walking with Sebak tells him, *"These people have grown to live for a long time because of their peace. Outside these walls there are people, elves, dwarves, etc. that can barely make it to forty years old. It's all sad and I wish someone would finally rise up and make a stand for everyone. That is what I pray for. I know I do not have the abilities capable of doing what needs to be done. What needs to be done requires a strong will to do what is right for the entire universe."*

He goes to speak to the druid that was just standing next to him and he has disappeared. Sebak was a little confused at what just transpired. He remembered walking out of the tower with one of the druids at his side. The rules were that he would always have to have an escort when he leaves the tower. Responsibly he goes back to the tower and informs them of what happened. They all were shocked at the information a little because of what Sebak said. They inform him, *"You were visited by the grand elder druid spirit. The first ever druid that ever walked the earth. He was a powerful and wise man that knew how to bring peace anywhere he went. That is the highest honor a druid could ever have."*

Meanwhile on the other side of the world, Alessia has traveled miles away from all the conflict and all the lies and deceit. It took her months to find somewhere she felt like was her home. She hiked for miles getting on ships and travelling alone without anyone to talk to. But she manages to find a place that she felt would make her feel wanted. She ends up in a cold mountain range with many fairies and other things that lived in harmony. There she finds the Vanir. Their presence warmed her soul to the very core. She was greeted by an arrestingly beautiful woman that welcomed her into her home. The mysterious woman said to Alessia. *"Greeting young one. How are you?"* Alessia responded, *"I am fine. Thanks for asking."*

Instantly the mysterious woman could sense all of Alessia's pain and suffering. She tuts at Alessia and says, *"Poor dear. I understand what you need. We can help you here if you want it?"* Alessia did not know what she was getting into but it couldn't be worse than what she has done before arriving here. She just agrees to take the mysterious woman's hospitality. Like Sebak days turned into weeks and weeks turned into months. She began to enjoy herself her in this world that she was in. She felt more accepted here and did not feel the weight of the world on her shoulders anymore. As if she could finally put her sword arm down forever.

After a few months go by Elurian teleports to the island to speak with Alessia. He greets her and the mysterious lady. He asks Alessia, *"How are you? How are things going for you?"* she replies with her normal answer. She says, *"I am fine Elurian. How is everything going over there?"* Before she could finish talking, he says, *"Sebak needs you. He doesn't admit it to anyone. But I can sense that he needs you."* Alessia is a little shocked that is why he came to see her today. She turns her back to Elurian and without looking him in the eye, she says, *"I don't care. He does not need me he is a grown man. he does not need me to hold his hand."* Elurian could not believe what he was hearing from her. In disgust he leaves through a portal.

Elurian leaves Alessia with disgust from what she said to him and tells her, *"I remember a time that you needed him and he was there without a second thought. Now that the roles are reversed, were is all that love now?"* then he steps through the portal and goes to check on another hero. He meets up with Neville to see how he is holding up. Neville says, *"Its not quiet. Nature is speaking about what is coming. I have had visions of the future. Many different outcomes. None of them end well. I'm not so sure about this Elurian. We are set on a path that has many roads. All those roads lead to something worse than the others. Us splitting up has started us down the roads that none can predict. We are just along for the ride now."* Elurian smirks at Neville because he can tell he is new at this.

"Its not fun is it waiting for something to happen? I have done that for centuries before Aethos and his children have made their moves. Their plans are always many moves ahead of me. I have always been too late to do anything about a situation but to engage the problem. The three of you have entered the biggest chess game in the universe. A game of life and death. One that these demons think is all fun and games. We have to stop them somehow. This cycle of hate and destruction must end somewhere." Elurian tells Neville. The two of them sitting on a huge branch of the world tree.

Neville thinks about what he was saying and began to piece together a plan.

He tells Elurian, *"One day there will be peace around this world. No more needless death and destruction. Just peace reigning around the world. one day there will be no need for armies and no need for guardians anymore. I dream of a day that I could walk through a village and see happy faces and not have to worry about any huge issues arising."* Elurian responds, *"That is a foolish dream and a selfish one. If these millennia of my life have taught me anything. There will always be some sort of conflict especially with humanity."*

Neville is confused by what Elurian was talking about and he personally felt like he had hated for humanity. Elurian could see the confusion in Neville's eyes and decides to show him. By using a little magic, he creates a small portal into the past for Neville to see what has happened. *"The elves and the other magical races would make their communities through voting and arguing. The Dwarves fought one another and so did the humans. But the humans did worse than the dwarves. The Dwarves would sanction fights for the crown. Humanity would have full on war and it would not end for years until someone relented. Their pride would cause many to starve and leave families scared from war. The humans with the crowns upon their heads did nothing for those that lost their lives in their wars."*

Neville watched in horror as Elurian also explained it to him. He stood corrected on the fact and felt horrible about the fact that he was about to start an argument with Elurian over that fact. But the proof was there in the history. Elurian says, *"I also don't want to bring it up but Sebak's father*

Bakari also sought war when he did not need to. Another human in history forcing their will on others to do their bidding." Neville felt a little more enlightened by the conversation as though his eyes were always closed to the history of humans. All he could say was, *"Wow you are right on a lot. You're like a walking history book."* He says with light humor.

"I hope we can finally end this with your generation." Elurian says. Neville replies, *"I hope we can to."* Elurian goes no to say, *"I do not think I could bare to watch the world die again. The first time almost destroyed me."* Neville was confused by the comment Elurian said. He goes to reiterate the comment, *"Yes son. I have watched the world be rebirth because Malborh had won before. I don't think we have enough strength to bare another rebirth of the planet. This is our last shot at stopping evil once and for all."*

EPILOGUE

Nine years passed; Neville decides that they are ready to act on a plan that he has taken nine years to prepare. He does not inform Elurian or any of the others what he was about to do. But he does recruit some druids that were willing to help him end all the bloodshed before it could begin. Neville gathers a few of the druids that are close to his age and he says to them, *"I do not want to wait for the enemy to destroy a village or a city. I want to end the bloodshed before it can actually begin. How is with me?"* eight druids agree to assist Neville in his personal mission to end the war on evil before it could really begin.

The nine of them weighted until the cover of night to draw an incantation upon the ground in an open area away from any villages or any life of any sort. They also draw a trap inside of the incantation to imprison whatever is summoned to the area. They all knew what they were doing was against the way the druids do things. They are not supposed to get involved directly unless necessary. But none of them wanted to watch villages be destroyed. They were all of one vision and it was to see the future without the demons. There was no turning back for them now. Everything was in place and Neville stood upon a rock to begin the spell.

The eight other druids surrounded the spell to make sure their trap was powerful against anything. Neville says the words to the spell and as his staff lights up, he slams it into the stone. Out of the sky comes a gigantic rock that floated towards the ground and into the trap. The spell was to summon one of the powerful demons to them inside the trap.

Before anyone could say anything, they hear this deep horrific growl coming from the rock inside the trap. Only to discover it wasn't a gigantic rock but a dragon balled up to look like a rock. The dragon roars loud enough for everyone in a hundred-mile radius could hear him. The dragon was black scaled and had four horns with red eyes. He says to them, *"Hello... Lunch."*

9 781951 300418